"I want you to be a part of my next project."

Matthew laughed out loud. "The one where you're planning to tie yourself to some poor louse with a ten-foot rope for thirty days and then dare him to touch you?"

"I simply want to make the point that men and women have more to offer one another than relief from hormonal needs," Jenny said.

"Hormonal needs?"

"Sex."

"And you think that if I'm tied to you for thirty days I'll come around to your point of view?"

"Yes, I do."

"Look, I know who I am and I know *what* I am. Who I am is a man. And what I am is attractive to women. I don't feel like spending the next thirty days fending you off."

"Don't worry, *sweetie pie—*"

His eyes narrowed in speculation. "You've got a deal."

MEN at WORK

✈—MILLIONAIRE'S CLUB   💼—BOARDROOM BOYS   ☀—MAGNIFICENT MEN
🐎—TALL, DARK & SMART   🍎—DOCTOR, DOCTOR   🗡—MEN OF THE WEST
🗡⚙ —MEN OF STEEL   🛡—MEN IN UNIFORM

MEN at WORK

JOAN JOHNSTON

FIT TO BE TIED

MAGNIFICENT MEN

Silhouette Books

Published by Silhouette Books

America's Publisher of Contemporary Romance

SILHOUETTE BOOKS
300 East 42nd St.,
New York, N.Y. 10017

ISBN 0-373-81034-2

FIT TO BE TIED

Copyright © 1988 by Joan Mertens Johnston

This edition published by arrangement with Harlequin Books S.A.

Printed in U.S.A.

Dear Reader,

I got the idea for *Fit To Be Tied* from an article I saw in the newspaper about an art project involving a couple tied together with an eight-foot rope for a year *who couldn't talk to each other!* Obviously I had to make some adjustments in that scenario to allow a romance to develop between my "chauvinist pig" Matthew Benson, and his nemesis, "feminist prig" Jennifer Smith. The world hasn't changed so much in the nearly ten years since this book was written. It's still necessary for men and women to compromise in order to live happily ever after...as Matt and Jenny will learn. Enjoy!

Best always,

Joan Johnston

Please address questions and book requests to:
Silhouette Reader Service
U.S.: 3010 Walden Ave., P.O. Box 1325, Buffalo, NY 14269
Canadian: P.O. Box 609, Fort Erie, Ont. L2A 5X3

Prologue

He'd been watching her for an hour, and it was beginning to make her nervous. Forty-five minutes ago he'd lit his first cigarette, and now she'd caught him throwing away the pack. Otherwise, he hadn't seemed nervous, just attentive as his gray eyes scanned her, then moved away to survey the other avant-garde art exhibits displayed in the small but prestigious SoHo gallery. She'd started to approach him at last, but he was joined by another man, who looked harried, rumpled and agitated, so she'd turned and edged away from the two of them. She felt the hairs rise on the back of her neck and shivered with anticipation. He was watching her again.

She'd been watching him for an hour, and it was beginning to make him nervous. He'd smoked a whole damn pack of cigarettes, trying to keep his mind off what he had to do, while he'd waited for George to arrive. The tall, slender woman appeared unperturbed by his study of her. Her eyes were huge and hazel, and they made his heart jump when he looked into them. That wasn't supposed to happen. He had work to do, and it was time he got to it. He didn't want to hurt her, but sometimes in his line of work he didn't have any choice.

One

I didn't expect her to be so feminine, not after everything I'd read about her. And her voice, so husky, as if she'd just finished drinking a whiskey straight up. I was right about what she does for a living, though. It's nothing a real woman ought to be doing, that's for damn sure.''

''Come on, Matt, don't you think you're being a little hard on her?''

Matthew Benson ran a quick hand through his shaggy black hair. ''I've been a critic for *Artist's World* a lot of years—''

''Long enough to have developed a less biased

outlook toward female artists," George chided. "As your friend—not to mention your editor—I think you're letting your personal feelings about Jennifer Smith get in the way of your professional opinion. She hasn't allowed her gender to get in the way of her art any more than any other artist would."

"Except that in Jennifer Smith's case her art is precisely aimed at making a *feminist* political statement. Women are as equal now as they're ever going to get. She's still fighting a battle that's already been conceded."

"I know a lot of women who wouldn't agree with you."

"Not any I'd want to know—your wife excepted, of course."

George frowned and picked a piece of lint off the rumpled cotton shirt he'd ironed that morning.

"You've been married to a liberated woman too long, old buddy," Matt accused. "I like my women big-eyed, full-busted, long-legged—"

"Addlepated—"

Matt grinned, and two long slashes that God had probably intended as dimples appeared on either side of his mouth. "Intelligence isn't absolutely necessary, but I never said I don't appreciate it."

"What about Jennifer Smith?"

"What about her?"

"What are you going to say in your review about the body-art performance we saw tonight in SoHo?"

"She certainly has the body for it," Matt quipped. "Big-eyed, full-busted, long-legged—"

George shook his head in disgust. "I can't believe you're not going to give her performance a fair review. You know how much clout *Artist's World* carries. Are you going to ruin her reputation as an artist because you don't agree with her politics?"

Matt's feet came down off his walnut desk, and he leaned over with his elbows braced on his knees. "I don't really object to performance art in principle," he said. "But when a beautiful young woman like Jennifer Smith spends a year as a bum on the New York City streets and labels it *Be All You Can Be*, I think somebody has to start drawing some lines."

Matt turned abruptly and shuffled through the stacks of paper on his desk until he found a copy of *Focus on Art*. "I found this article on her by accident." He threw the magazine into George's lap with such force that the other man had to grapple to catch it.

"Her next project is to spend a month tied to a man by a ten-foot rope without touching him. You know why? To prove that the sexes can be separate but equal!"

Matt grabbed the magazine back before George had a chance to locate the article and slammed it down on his desk. "With the right man, she wouldn't last ten seconds in that situation."

"A man such as yourself?"

"Damn right."

"Then why don't you volunteer for the job?"

"I've got better things to do with my time than spend it proving my point to a feminist prig!"

"Sounds to me like a chauvinist pig and a feminist prig ought to get along together just fine," George countered.

"Very funny." Matt leaned back in his swivel chair and settled the heels of his expensive Italian shoes on his desk. He pulled a cigarette from the pack in the breast pocket of his stiffly starched shirt and lit it with the silver lighter he'd bought to celebrate his final divorce decree.

"You still haven't told me how you plan to review the performance we just saw," George said.

"You'll have to wait and read it tomorrow morning," Matt answered. "Now go home to your wife and let me get to work."

"I'm here to see Matthew Benson."

The *Artist's World* receptionist had strict orders from Matt to put off women such as the one who stood before her now: blond, beautiful and buxom, with pouting lips that begged to be kissed, and huge eyes that declared both innocence and womanly intent. It was the slender woman's proud stance and exotic attire that caused the receptionist to pause for a moment before issuing the automatic rejection Matt had dictated. The woman's cream-colored silk blouse buttoned all the way to the neck, but tatters of cloth that looked as though a cat had run its claws through the material were all that remained of the sleeves, which hung in ragged ribbons from her shoulders. Her fitted black silk trousers had the same ragged effect from the knee down. This woman was clearly different from the norm. But orders were orders. "I'm sorry. Unless you have an appointment—"

"He'll see me. Tell him Jennifer Smith wants to talk with him about his review of *Woman at a Party*," she said with cool, businesslike authority.

The receptionist recognized the name immediately. "It's nice to meet you, Miss Smith."

"That's *Ms.* Smith."

"Yes, so sorry..." The receptionist looked over her shoulder across the roomful of personal computers to a few private, glass-walled cubicles along the far back wall. "He's in. I'll let him know you're here."

The receptionist punched out a number and spoke quietly into the phone, then said, "He'll see you. He's back in that far corner."

Jenny saw a hand waving in one of the cubicles and assumed it was Matthew Benson. Rotten chauvinist. Destroyer of artistic careers. Heartless creep. She crumpled the most recent copy of *Artist's World* more tightly in her hand and strode quickly toward his office before she lost her nerve.

He met her at the door, and for a moment Jenny wasn't sure she could go through with what she'd planned. But then she remembered the harsh words he'd written. She lifted her chin, swallowed and asked, "Are you Matthew Benson?"

"Yes. Please come in, Miss Smith."

"It's Ms. Smith."

"Please come in, *Ms*. Smith," Matt repeated, smiling patronizingly. He held a chair out for her like a gentleman should, waiting for her to seat herself.

"I'll stand, thank you," she said. "This isn't going to take long."

"Fine. I hope you won't mind, then, if I sit?"

"Not at all." She watched him settle his tall body comfortably in the swivel chair behind his desk. He looked different from the shaggy-haired man who'd watched her so intensely at the SoHo gallery, the

man who'd smiled at her and made her neck hairs
rise with anticipation.

She guessed he was probably in his mid-thirties,
at least five years older than she was, but he was
obviously a prime physical specimen. He'd rolled
the sleeves of his Oxford cloth shirt up to reveal
muscular forearms, loosened the top button of his
shirt, and pulled the knot of his tie down, exposing
a tuft of curly black hair at his throat. His shoulders
filled the back of his chair from side to side, yet she
noticed his waist was narrow and his stomach flat.
She couldn't find one fault with his finely-honed
male body, but then, she wasn't here to complain
about his looks.

"What's on your mind, honey?" he said, consciously needling her.

Jenny bristled at the condescending address and
slammed the battered magazine down on his littered
desk. The pages caught the edge of one of several
Styrofoam coffee cups and sent it flying.

"Look out!"

Jenny's warning came too late. Even Matt's quick
reflexes as he jumped up in response to her cry
weren't able to save his lightweight pleated pants
from a dousing. He swore every oath he knew as he
swiped at his trousers, trying to get rid of the excess

coffee, most of which had landed in an embarrass-ingly personal spot.

Acting on reflex, Jenny raced to help. She grabbed a crumpled napkin from the desk and used it to pat him dry as best she could, even though he kept backing away from her as she worked. Sud-denly he seemed to be choking, and Jenny looked up to see what else could have happened to the poor man.

He wasn't choking, he was laughing. Or rather, trying not to laugh. "If you'd wanted a chance to check me out, *Ms.* Smith, I would have been glad to oblige. You didn't have to spill coffee in my lap."

Jenny looked down again and realized that her hand was spread across the front of his trousers. The soaked napkin that, together with a thin layer of damp material, was all that separated her from his flesh, wasn't hot. It wasn't even lukewarm. He'd never been in any danger of getting scalded.

Jenny dropped the napkin, which landed with a splat at Matt's feet, and backed around the desk, her hands balled into fists, her face fiery red. She was so upset she couldn't even enjoy the ridiculous sight the Great Matthew Benson presented to her.

Matt stood there for a moment, pretending a non-chalance he didn't feel. The truth was, her touch had affected him more than he cared to admit, and in a moment that was going to become readily apparent to her. In an attempt to salvage what little dignity he could from the situation, he quickly seated himself behind the concealing desk and leaned his forearms across it imposingly.

"All right, *lady*," he said, a snide grin revealing even white teeth. "Say what you have to say and then get the hell out of here so I can go change my clothes."

Matt's aggressive attitude immediately squelched the remorse Jenny had been feeling for the disaster she'd caused. If he wanted to ignore what had happened and talk business, then she'd talk business. She straightened to her full, not inconsiderable, height and said, "I think your review of *Woman at a Party* was unfair, especially the part where you define my support of women's rights as 'rehashing rotten eggs and spoiled corned beef.'"

"It's my opinion that you're dredging up old issues. Your subject is outdated and stale. Like moldy bread. Or soggy crackers. Your art just isn't relevant, *Ms.* Smith."

Jenny clenched her fists even tighter and tried to remain unmoved by his smug condemnation of her work. After all, it was only one man's opinion, with *man* as the operative word. "You're wrong, and I'd like to suggest a way I can prove it to you."

"Lady, if you think you can change my mind about anything right now—"

"I want you to be a part of my next project." She spoke quickly to get everything said while his mouth was still hanging open. "If we spend thirty days together without touching—that is, if we prove my premise that the sexes can be separate but equal—I want you to print a retraction of your statements about *Woman at a Party*."

He said nothing for another moment. Then he laughed out loud. "You want me to be a part of your project? The one where you're planning to tie yourself to some poor louse with a ten-foot rope for thirty days and then dare him to touch you?"

Jenny swallowed hard as his eyes skimmed her body from head to toe. She felt stripped and reached up to check whether the button on her neckline was closed. It was. She patted the tight French twist that contained her silky blond hair. Every strand was safely in place. So what was he looking at? "You make it sound as though I'm issuing a challenge to the male sex," she said. "It isn't like that at all."

"Oh, yeah?"

"Yeah—yes. I simply want to make the point that men and women have more to offer to one another than relief from hormonal needs."

"Hormonal needs?"

"Sex."

"And you think that if I'm tied to you for thirty days I'll come around to your point of view?"

"Yes, I do."

Matt stood and leaned across the desk with his palms braced on the paper-strewn surface. "Hell will freeze over first."

Jenny found herself hard-pressed to hold her position, because now his face was less than a foot from hers, and his gray eyes had locked with her hazel ones, causing havoc with her pulse. With a straight face she said, "They say the polar ice cap is moving south a few inches every day."

Matt laughed and stood straight again, relieving the unaccountable tension—surely not sexual—that had risen between them. "You seem pretty sure of my behavior, *Ms.* Smith. What about your own? What do I get if you can't keep your hands off me for the full thirty days?"

"If—and it's a pretty big if—I should be the one to touch you first, or if I should ask you to touch me, then naturally I wouldn't be entitled to the retraction. But—" Jenny's eyes turned flinty "—I wouldn't count on that happening. I assure you, I find nothing about you the least bit tempting."

Matt laughed. "That's too bad. Some women find me quite attractive."

Jenny would have sneered at his arrogance, except at that moment she felt the same shiver of anticipation run through her that she'd felt when he'd watched her at the SoHo gallery. "I assume you can control your sexual appetite for thirty days."

"I'm so certain I could control myself with you that if I lost on that score, I'd print a retraction of my opinions about your art so fast it would make your head spin. Not that I've agreed to this idiocy," he qualified.

He strolled around the desk and leaned back with his narrow hips against the edge of it, crossing his arms so his biceps bulged beneath the Oxford cloth.

Unconsciously, Jenny backed up a step. She very carefully didn't look down at his wet trousers.

He grinned at her knowingly. "You still have to give me one good reason why I should agree to tie myself to a woman for thirty days with the stipulation that we can't touch one another."

"Because you think you're right. And because you want to prove me wrong."

She was perceptive. Matt granted her that. He appreciated the ingenious simplicity of her appeal. "Even if I were inclined to take you up on this ridiculous proposition, there's no way I could get the time off to follow through with it," he said at last.

"I talked to your editor, George Taplinger, this morning before I came here. Mr. Taplinger said he thought it was a wonderful idea, and that he'd be glad to give you the time off to do it. He said there were only a few exhibits you'd have to cover, and of course he'd expect you to do a review and a short article on my project when it was over."

"George agreed to this?"

"He did."

"He would," Matt muttered under his breath. "How is this supposed to work? What happens when I want to pursue activities you're not interested in doing—exercise, movies, football games?"

"I'll come along with you," Jenny explained. "Of course, when I teach my classes at the New School, you'll come along with me."

"Of course. So we'd do everything together?"

"So long as we didn't have to touch, yes. And with the understanding that we'll allow each other as much personal privacy as possible."

Matt smiled, the feral look of an animal who knows it has its quarry cornered. "You know, I'd almost be inclined to agree to do this, if it weren't for some personal plans I have coming up this month. If you know what I mean."

"Would these plans entail spending time with an-

other woman?'' Jenny inquired with a nonchalance
she wasn't feeling.

"Exactly."

"Our arrangement wouldn't have to interfere with
that."

"No?"

"The prohibition on touching is only for you and
me. What other woman, or women, you choose
to…touch during the term of this project is your
business."

"And you won't mind?"

Jenny blushed. "I suspect there will be many
times when we'll wish for more privacy than we
have. I've resigned myself to it."

"For the sake of art," he intoned.

"Yes."

"Look, this whole project strikes me as so much
baloney. I know who I am, and I know *what* I am.
Who I am is a man. And what I am is attractive to
women. I don't feel like spending the next thirty
days fending you off."

Jenny could tell he was goading her, could tell he
wanted her to refuse to have him as her partner for
the project. But after the review he'd just written,
she knew the only way to convince him that the
feminist statements she made through her art had
validity was to make him come with her and live

for thirty days in her shadow. When he saw the world through her eyes, perhaps he'd better understand what she hoped to accomplish through her art. She needed that retraction. Her credibility with her peers depended on it.

"Don't worry, *sweetie pie*," Jenny said. "I want that retraction, and you don't want to give it to me. That ought to be enough to keep both of us at the ends of our rope. So what do you say, Mr. Benson?"

"Make it Matt," he said with a teasing wink. "Have you ever lived with a man, *Ms.* Smith?"

"Make it Jenny," she said. "And yes, I have."

"And you don't find the situation you propose just a little, well, titillating?"

"I'm certain I could live platonically with a man, if that's what you're asking. I lived platonically with my husband for several months before our divorce."

Matt heard the bitterness in her voice. "Is that why you hate men? Because your husband didn't desire you physically?"

"I don't hate—" Jenny bit off her response. She felt the blood leave her face as she struggled for a suitable response to Matt's inquiry. "I think it would be better if we leave personal feelings out of this," she said finally.

"He was a fool," Matt said.

"What?" she breathed.

"And so am I for doing this." His eyes narrowed in speculation before he said, "All right, you've got a deal."

Jenny stood in stunned surprise for a moment before she realized what he'd said. "You'll do it?"

"Sure. Why not?"

She reached for the hand he'd extended to her and concentrated on denying the frisson of sexual awareness she felt at his touch. "There's one other thing, Mr. Benson."

"Matt," he said with a dazzling smile.

"Matt," she repeated, making her voice stern. "I've agreed to display my performance art at a different gallery for each of the next four weeks. We'll be traveling to San Francisco, Chicago and Houston, and then finish up here in New York the last weekend of the project."

"Damn! I should have realized—"

"You aren't backing out, are you, Matt?" she asked sweetly.

At that moment George stuck his head in the door. "How are you two getting along?"

"Swell," Matt said. "Do you realize what you've just gotten me into?"

"The decision was entirely yours," George said with a grin. "I take it Jenny persuaded you to participate in her project."

"All I need to know is where and when to show up," he said, turning to Jenny expectantly.

"My apartment, 7:00 a.m., day after tomorrow. We begin September 1 and finish September 30—*if* you can last that long." She spun on her heel and headed for the door.

"I can't imagine why any woman would work so hard to prove she can be equal to a man," Matt said to her back.

Jenny had already reached the door but turned to reply, "Neither can I. A woman who only wants to be equal to a man doesn't have much ambition." And then she was gone.

"Guess she got in the last word, all right," George remarked.

Matt sat back down at his desk and put his feet up, reaching into his pocket for a cigarette. "The game's just beginning," he replied, "And as a famous sports*man* once said, 'It ain't over 'til it's over.'"

Two

Jenny had a nervous stomach. And a sick head. And goose bumps for good measure, since she had never believed in doing anything halfway. It was 6:45 a.m. September 1, and any moment Matthew Benson was going to come through her front door. To say she was anxious would have been to underestimate her condition. Panicked was more like it.

She practiced *the knot* again, the one that was going to bind her to Matt Benson for thirty full days...and nights. If only he were a less obvious chauvinist. If only she weren't such a determined feminist. She wished she'd never considered using Matt Benson as her partner in this project.

Jenny hadn't always been a feminist. In fact, the exact opposite had been true until she'd married Sam. Jenny had wanted nothing more in life than to marry and have babies. But when Sam hadn't earned enough money to support the children they'd both wanted, she'd gone out and gotten a job. She hadn't earned much when she'd started working at the small public relations firm in downtown Houston, but even that invasion of Sam's territory had been the beginning of the end of their marriage.

Due to circumstances neither of them could control, he had lost his job just as she'd gotten her third promotion. He'd asked her to quit because he needed to be the breadwinner, the king of the castle. But by then she was pregnant, and it was either keep working or lose her health insurance. Sam had told her to get rid of the baby. They could have another one later on, when he could afford to pay for it.

It was then that Jenny had realized a husband wasn't necessarily the Prince Charming she'd read about in fairy tales, nor even the hero glorified in romances. She hadn't gotten rid of the baby; she'd gotten rid of Sam instead. It had been agonizing to divorce him, and that hadn't been the end of the pain.

Her employer had demanded she quit her job when he found out she was pregnant, then refused to rehire her after the baby came. She protested. She might have won a lawsuit, but Jenny hadn't had the money or the emotional energy to sue. She suddenly found herself labeled a feminist and a liberated woman. She didn't care much for the labels, but she believed a woman ought to have the same opportunities as a man.

To her, that meant a woman had the right to be as intelligent, as assertive, as successful and as demanding of herself as any man. It didn't mean she wasn't also a woman—which was why she was sorry she'd agreed to spend the next thirty days tied to Matt Benson. Because unhappy as it made her to admit the fact, Jenny was attracted to the man.

"Hey, in there. Anybody home?"

Jenny started unlocking chains on the first knock, but in New York you couldn't be too careful, so it was almost a full minute before she opened the door to Matt Benson's devastating smile. A well-worn traveling bag was slung carelessly over his brawny shoulder.

"Here I am. What took you so long to open the door? Weren't you expecting me to show up?" he asked as he stepped inside.

"Yes, of course, but—"

"—in New York you can't be too careful," he finished with an understanding smile as he eyed the large selection of locks and bolts on Jenny's door.

She was appalled to find him so cheerful. She was never going to last thirty days if he kept smiling at her like that, with those dimples in his cheeks turned to creases. He was wearing jeans that fit him in all the right places and a cable knit cotton sweater that emphasized his broad shoulders. His hair was windblown and as endearingly shaggy as ever. She wanted to touch him, and that was exactly what she couldn't do for the next thirty days.

Jenny followed the path of Matt's traveling bag as it came off his shoulder and slid down the length of his jeans-clad legs to the floor. She was still staring at his shiny brown loafers when he demanded, "Well, would you care to show me around first, honey? Or do we tie the knot right now?"

Flustered by her unruly emotions, Jenny reacted to Matt's chauvinistic form of address with a pert, "Right now we get a few things straight. The first is that I'm not your *honey*!"

"My mistake, hon—Ms. Smith."

Jenny was suspicious of his easy capitulation, and also disgusted, because she could have used an argument to ease the tension between them. She took a quick look at her watch. 6:48. "We have a few minutes. It might be easier if I show you everything before we start. Follow me.''

Matt would have followed her anywhere. Her jeans molded her fanny the way he wanted his hands to, and her generous breasts swayed beneath the sleeveless cotton-knit shirt she wore. How on earth was he going to keep his side of this bargain? By God, he'd make her so hot she'd *beg* him to touch her…if he didn't go down in flames first himself.

She walked a step or two into the room, then gestured with outspread arms at a beige open-weave couch accented with nubby throw pillows. Nearby sat a bamboo swivel chair and a round glass-topped table, with the latest art magazines arranged carefully on top. ''This is the living area.'' She swept a hand toward the other side of the large room, where a wooden table and two wooden chairs stood guarded by a white stove, refrigerator and sink. ''That's the kitchen and dining room.''

''I guessed that.'' He looked around the room again, noting the dark, dragon-patterned Oriental rug covering the shiny hardwood floors. ''No TV?''

''Do you watch much TV?'' she asked.

''I've been known to catch a football game here and there, and the occasional women's mud-wrestling program.''

Jenny snorted at the blatancy of his macho preferences. "Of course."

"Well?"

Jenny crossed to a floor-to-ceiling oak unit along one wall and opened a set of folding doors. "The TV's in here."

Matt joined her at the cabinet and started opening more doors.

"What are you looking for now?"

"A stereo?" he asked hopefully.

"Sorry," she said, shaking her head. "Lost it in the divorce and just never got around to getting another one. I do have an AM-FM radio. Think you can manage to survive?"

"When in Rome…" He shrugged nonchalantly, but quickly began checking the titles of the books in her cupboard before she could close the doors.

Other than the art reference works that Jenny would naturally have in her library, Matt was confused by what he found. Not that he was surprised to see the serious books about women's issues, but what he hadn't expected to find was the large collection of romance novels. What kind of woman spent half her time reading books devoted to proving how badly men treated women and the other half reading about heroes and heroines and Happily Ever After?

Jenny saw the furrow between Matt's brows and quickly closed the doors on her small library. Well, what had he expected? Steinbeck? Shakespeare? Dostoyevsky? "Come on. I'll show you the rest." Jenny headed through a doorway to the bedroom. "We'll be sleeping in here."

In the bedroom Matt discovered twin beds with a narrow rattan nightstand between them. The bedspreads were light beige, and the lamp on the nightstand was the same navy as the plain carpet on the hardwood floor. Where was the splash of color in her life?

Jenny opened a closet to show Matt the space she'd made for him, and he found the answer to his question. Jenny's clothes reflected a rainbow of color. He gazed at the pink shirt and blue jeans she wore. He could hardly wait to see her dressed in the purples and oranges and reds he'd seen in the closet.

"...and I've cleared a drawer for you in the chest," she finished. "Are the accommodations all right?"

Matt realized he hadn't been paying attention. But the truth was that there was only one aspect of their accommodations he cared about in the least. He nodded his head toward the twin beds. "We certainly won't have to worry about bumping into one another at night, will we?"

"No we won't," Jenny replied succinctly. She checked her watch. 6:52. "There's more to see, and we're running out of time."

Jenny had wanted him to like her home, but she could tell he was disappointed. What was missing? Surely he wasn't sulking because she didn't have a stereo. Jenny's mouth twisted in an expression of disbelief. He hadn't really expected both of them to sleep in the same bed, had he?

"Bathroom's here." Jenny opened a door off the bedroom to a small cubicle that contained a sink, commode and tub, all white and spotlessly shiny.

She showed him the hole she'd chiseled in the door frame so the rope that tied them together could run through it when the bathroom door was shut. She turned back to face him. "That's it."

He looked around the room again and realized there were no personal things on the nightstand or the low clothes chest except a bottle of very expensive perfume. In a feminist's bedroom? He'd thought they were into natural scents. Or maybe that was environmentalists. He casually strolled a little closer to Jenny and took a deep breath, trying to find out if she was wearing any of the perfume. She turned abruptly and caught him sniffing. He almost choked trying to stop.

Jenny frowned with concern. "Are you all right?"

"Uh." That was intelligent. "Fine. It all looks very…neat," he added with a total lack of savoir faire.

"Thank you."

Actually, he mused, the apartment was astonishingly neat. No, neat was too simple a word. Immaculate. Nothing seemed to be out of place. It didn't quite look, well, lived in. It made him nervous. No lint on the carpet. No dustballs in the corners. No layer of life on the furniture. No butts in the—Good God! *No ashtrays!*

"I don't see any ashtrays."

"I don't smoke," Jenny replied.

He made his voice stern. "I do."

"Not in this apartment, you don't." Jenny pointed to a sign that said, Thank You For Not Smoking.

It took him a moment to realize the sign was in her bedroom. He felt a moment of insane, irrational jealousy. Just exactly who wasn't allowed to smoke in Jennifer Smith's bedroom? He only said, "We're going to talk about this."

Jenny looked at her watch. 6:55. "Talk fast. Patrick should be here any minute."

"Patrick?"

"He's the photographer."

Matt let that pass for the moment because she was looking at her watch again. "Surely you knew I smoked when you asked me to participate in this project."

"Cigarettes aren't good for you," she countered.

"That's beside the point."

"You should quit."

"Jenny…" he warned.

"All right! You should cut down."

He shook his head in exasperation.

"Don't you care about your health?" she demanded.

"I always smoke a cigarette to relax before I go to bed at night." When she opened her mouth to retort, he added, "It helps to keep my blood pressure down."

"I'd be willing to sit outside on the front stoop with you while you smoke your evening cigarette," she offered.

He grimaced. Normally he could manage with only the occasional cigarette. But he'd been known to chain-smoke an entire pack in tension-fraught situations. He was quite sure the next thirty days would qualify as such, and she'd just made it clear he was going to have an argument every time he used cigarettes to relieve the tension. "I'm going to kill George," he muttered.

The knock on the front door sent them both back to the living room. Jenny unlocked the door and welcomed Patrick Stuart with a warm smile.

The first thing Matt saw was the pack of cigarettes in Patrick's pocket. The second thing he saw was the bulky camera he carried.

"He's the one taking pictures?" Matt asked.

"Patrick will be photographing the project at intervals. He's doing a paper on social realism in art," Jenny explained. "My project qualifies as a contemporary example of the use of art to express social values."

Matt took another look at the exceptionally tall, exceptionally well-built, exceptionally handsome young man. He had eyes as blue as the Caribbean, sun-bleached blond hair, and a smile that was blinding against his healthy tan. Matt would have sworn he was younger than Jenny Smith by a couple of years, but then, he didn't suppose that would stop a liberated woman like her.

"Patrick Stuart, this is Matthew Benson, the critic for *Artist's World*," Jenny said. "Matt, this is Patrick Stuart, my brightest and most talented student."

Intelligence and talent, too? Even worse, it was obvious the young man knew his way around the apartment. Matt stuck out his hand. Never let it be said that Matt Benson couldn't handle a little competition. "Hello, Patrick. It's nice to meet you."

"The pleasure's mine," Patrick said. "I read your reviews all the time, and I respect your opinion, sir."

The younger man's grip was strong, his voice sincere. It was hard not to like Patrick Stuart. "Make it Matt," Matt said, smiling back at the other man.

Jenny looked at her watch. 6:58. "Guess this is it. Patrick, get your camera ready." Jenny picked up the half-inch thick white rope lying on the couch and turned to Matt. "Would you lift up your sweater so I can tie this around your waist?"

Matt hadn't thought much about where the rope was going to be tied. Now he realized there was no place except their waists that would still allow them to change their clothes on a regular basis. He reached down and pulled his sweater halfway up, exposing his abdomen.

Jenny had to reach with both hands to bring the rope around his trim waist, and it forced her face against his chest. She couldn't breathe without inhaling the intoxicating male scent of him. The cable knit was soft against her cheek, and beneath it she could feel the hard strength of his body. She worked quickly, disturbed by the enforced closeness. She

handed the rope from one hand to the other around
his back and brought it to his stomach to tie *the knot*.

Jenny hadn't really allowed herself to look at the
skin he'd exposed. As she tied the knot, she had no
choice. His abdomen was striated with hard muscle,
and the curly hair on his chest arrowed into a single
line of downy black hair that disappeared into his
jeans. He wasn't wearing a belt, and his pants had
slid down on his hips until they'd caught on his
hipbones. If he was wearing any underwear, she
didn't see any signs of it. Jenny shivered. Every time
she moved the rope her knuckles brushed his belly,
and he sucked it in so his muscles rippled under her
touch. The next few moments were agonizing. Her
hands felt like clumsy leaden weights, and her stomach fluttered unaccountably.

Once she'd finished tying the knot, Jenny stepped
back with a sigh of relief and said, "All done."

"Thank God," Matt said under his breath. She'd
known what she was doing, the little tease. If she'd
glanced down she would have gotten a pretty good
idea of how successful she'd been. Well, two could
play this game. He picked up the other end of the
rope. "Your turn."

"I can do it," Jenny said, reaching for the rope.

Matt held it out of her grasp. "Turnabout's fair
play."

Jenny dropped her hand, caught off guard by the mischievous look in his eyes.

"Now, any special kind of knot you want?" he asked.

"Whatever. Just make sure it's snug, but not too tight."

"Lift your shirt then, will you?" he said.

Jenny reached down and gathered the loose cotton folds of her shirt under her breasts. When Matt reached around her, his face was right beside hers, and she could feel his moist breath on her ear. She'd chosen the kind of cord often used to hold back draperies, and the rope felt silky against her waist. The hairs on Matt's arm brushed against her skin, and she shivered at the touch of his fingertips as he slowly secured the knot.

Matt couldn't believe how soft her skin was. He wanted to reach up under the shirt and cup her breasts in his hands, to take the nipple he could see tightening under the flimsy material into his mouth and suck it until she moaned. He wanted to put his tongue in her ear and feel her shiver in his arms. He would do it all, he vowed. And before the damned thirty days were up! He contented himself with brushing his knuckles across her abdomen and "accidentally" dropping his thumb into her belly button for a teasing caress. He took a quick look and found her eyes dilated and her nostrils flaring. Oh, she was a woman, all right. And he would take her like one of the heroes in her romance novels before he was through.

"There. All done," he said, his voice husky.

They were both breathing heavily by the time he'd finished, and only belatedly became aware that Patrick had been snapping pictures the entire time. Jenny looked up at Matt and got caught by a flash. She let her eyes adjust and checked her watch. 7:00 a.m. on the nose. "All right, Patrick. It's time for one last picture. Step as far away from me as you can, Matt. Let the rope extend as far as it will."

Matt took one, two, three steps away. Jenny had carefully measured the rope to be sure that after it was tied around both their waists it would still give them the desired ten feet of distance from one another. She'd walked off ten feet in her living room and knew it wasn't very far. It seemed even closer with Matt on the other end of the rope.

"Are you ready for a picture?" Patrick asked.

Jenny took a deep, calming breath. "Yes. Yes, I am. Matt, how about you?"

The rope around his waist burned into his skin as he said, "Yes. I'm ready."

Patrick adjusted the wide-angle lens and snapped

the picture. "I'd better get going now. I want to develop this film before class today."

"I'll see you at nine," Jenny said as she closed the door behind him.

"Do you teach today?" Matt asked.

"Half days Tuesdays and Thursdays," she replied. "A class in art history and one on contemporary women artists."

"And you can make enough doing that to live?"

"I have another source of income."

She didn't elaborate, and he couldn't bring himself to ask. "How about a cup of coffee?" he suggested.

"I don't drink it," Jenny replied.

Matt groaned.

"I've got tea."

"No thanks." He needed a cigarette.

"Maybe we can go shopping later today and get some coffee and a percolator," she offered.

"Yeah. Great."

"Can I offer you a toasted waffle?" When he stared at her aghast, Jenny stiffened her spine and said, "I don't like to cook. But mostly I don't like to wash dishes. If you want a more elaborate breakfast, you're welcome to cook it and clean up after yourself."

Matt would have starved first. "I'll take the waffle. You can make it."

Since they were already as far from one another as the rope would allow, the moment Matt moved toward the kitchen Jenny was pulled along behind him. He felt the tug at his waist and stopped. He turned and cocked a questioning brow. "You coming?"

"I guess I don't have much choice," Jenny muttered. It was done. They were tied by an umbilical cord for the next thirty days.

Matt sat at the kitchen table while Jenny took two waffles out of the freezer and popped them into the toaster.

"They smell like they're burning," he said a few minutes later.

"You want to cook?"

Matt shook his head.

"Then don't complain." When the waffles popped up, Jenny plopped them down on a plate and handed them to Matt with a package of butter and a plastic container of syrup. "Eat hearty."

Matt eyed the waffles suspiciously, but they turned out to be surprisingly good.

"Who cooks for you at home?" Jenny asked as she watched him wolf his food down.

"I usually eat out. Or someone cooks for me."

Jenny had a feeling "someone" translated into "a woman I'm dating." "Why don't you learn how to cook?"

"I know how to cook."

"You do? When did you learn? Who taught you?"

Matt smiled sardonically. "My mother taught me."

"What?"

"She was a busy woman. Much too busy to cook breakfast for the family. So she taught me how to do it."

"How big a family?"

"Five brothers and two sisters."

"I was an only child," Jenny volunteered, then asked, "Were you the eldest?"

"Sure was."

"What else did your mother teach you?"

"I do a mean tub of laundry, I'm hell on wheels with a vacuum, and I can change a diaper in four seconds flat."

He was smiling when he said it, but somehow she knew he wasn't kidding. "So when did you become a male chauvinist pig?"

He laughed. It was a booming sound, full of warmth, and it made her blood run fast to hear it.

"You liberated women don't pull any punches, do you?"

"No. Are you going to answer my question?"

His face sobered. "When I got married. No. When I got divorced."

"Oh."

He played with the rope that lay on the table between them as he spoke. "My wife, Adrienne, was the consummate career woman. She chewed me up and spit me out like a toothpick." He paused and ran a hand through his hair, rumpling it even more. "I was in and out of that marriage so fast I didn't even know what hit me. When we split, she took me for every dime I had. So much for liberated women being able to support themselves."

"I'm sorry," she said.

"It was a long time ago, and I learned my lesson. I won't be so quick to tie myself to another woman."

It took a second for him to realize what he'd said, and then he grinned ruefully. "Tie myself *permanently* to another woman," he corrected.

Jenny took that to mean he was no longer interested in marrying. Well, neither was she.

"I'm done," he announced, sitting back in his chair.

"Done?"

"You can take these dishes away now."

This time it was Jenny's turn to laugh. "Remember me? The liberated woman? I don't do dishes. You can stack them in the dishwasher."

Matt narrowed his eyes, wondering how serious she was.

"We're both equals here," Jenny elaborated. "That means you do your fair share. I made the meal. You do the dishes."

Matt grimaced. "Is that the best deal I'm going to get?"

"It's the only deal you're going to get."

"In that case, excuse me." Matt stood and shoved the sleeves of his cable-knit sweater up to his elbows before carrying his dishes to the sink to rinse them.

Jenny marveled at the strength she saw in his arms and wondered, not for the first time, how he stayed in shape. Maybe she'd find out over the next thirty days. His jeans hugged his taut buttocks, and she had a mental picture of her hands cupping them and sliding down to his rock-hard thighs, which would be covered with the same curly hair as his forearms and chest.

Abruptly she sat up straight, her face flushed with embarrassment as she began one of her typical arguments with herself.

Shame on you, Jennifer Smith!

What did I do wrong?

The only reason Matthew Benson set foot through that front door in the first place is so you could prove that a man can treat a woman as more than a sexual object—and vice versa. Just look at you! Only 7:42, and you're already ogling Matt Benson's buns!

You have to admit they're nice—

Jennifer!

All right, all right! I'll start appreciating his male chauvinist mind, if you'd prefer it.

I most certainly do prefer it!

Matt saw the cantankerous expression on Jenny's face the moment he turned around. He decided to ignore it. He wiped his hands with a dishtowel and asked, "How soon before we have to leave for campus?"

He watched Jenny check her watch and realized how bound she was to the clock. Didn't she ever do anything without looking to see what time it was?

"I guess it wouldn't hurt to arrive a little early today," Jenny said. "My class is excited about the project, and they'll want to meet you before we get started. We can leave anytime you're ready."

He threw the dishtowel on the table. "I'm ready now."

Jenny picked up the towel as she stood, and

folded it as she walked over to rehang it on the rack by the sink. "Dishtowels go here when they're not being used," she instructed.

Matt needed a cigarette. He smiled to cover his irritation and asked, "Are you going to spend the next thirty days picking up after me?"

She smiled to cover her own irritation and asked, "Are you going to spend the next thirty days dropping things all over this apartment?"

Neither one said anything for a moment, and the tension arced between them like an electrical current.

Matt took a deep breath and then exhaled, searching for the right words to say what he thought he *had* to say. "I agreed to participate in your project, Jenny, but I didn't agree to change who I am. So if I drop something, you'll have to decide whether it bothers you more to pick it up or let it lie. I have no intention of tiptoeing around worrying about whether I've broken one of your unspoken rules. For the next thirty days this is my home, too, and I'm going to treat it as such. Now, do you want to call this off right now, or do we go on from here?"

Jenny looked at her watch. 7:57. Three minutes short of an hour together and they were already at each other's throats.

"Let's—"

Call it off right now, Jennifer. How will you ever be able to stand a whole month of that kind of high-handedness?

He isn't being so unreasonable, really. How would you feel if the circumstances were reversed and you were staying at his place?

Can you even imagine the chaos that must exist at his place?

That's beside the point.

That's exactly the point. How will your apartment look after he's spent thirty days dropping his undershorts beside the bed?

Jenny smiled at the picture that thought conjured up.

"All right, Matt. I'll try not to pick up after you any more than I can help. Will that satisfy you?"

"And you won't try to change any more of my habits?" he insisted.

"And I won't try to change any more of your habits," Jenny agreed.

She couldn't wait to see that pile of undershorts beside his bed.

Three

Jenny's students were as excited to be able to witness her performance art project as she'd thought they would be, and they spent almost half the class asking Matt questions about what it was like to be an art critic. Jenny was impressed by how astutely he answered and had to admit he hadn't gotten where he was by accident. When she began her lecture, he sat down in a chair near the podium to be out of the way.

Jenny hadn't realized how much she paced in the classroom, or how often she moved in close to her students to make a point. Her rope only gave her three short strides before she was pulled up short. The third time she found herself stopped so abruptly, Matt grinned ruefully at her, set the chair aside and stood near the blackboard, ready to move when she did in order to give her the freedom to teach.

When the class was over and her students had all left, Jenny turned to him and said a simple but heartfelt, "Thank you."

"I'm sure you would have done the same for me," he replied. "And you were doing such a good job teaching, I hated to be in the way."

Jenny turned away to hide her blush of pleasure at the compliment.

Matt continued, "I was especially intrigued by the problem you gave them to think about for next Tuesday. I have to admit, I wouldn't want to have to choose whether to rescue the *Mona Lisa* or an old, sick man from a burning building. How would you solve the dilemma?"

"For a lot of years I saved the painting."

Matt's eyes widened in astonishment before he saw the beginning of her wry smile. "And now?"

She shrugged. "I grew up. I've seen more of life's ups and downs." The smile grew wider as she added, "And I've lost my fondness for the *Mona Lisa*. How about you? Would you save the old man or the painting?"

"You gave the class until Tuesday to think about it. Don't I get the same consideration?"

"All right. But I'll be looking forward to hearing what you have to say." Jenny checked her watch. "It's nearly lunchtime. Are you hungry?"

"A little. You must have worked up quite an appetite with all that pacing in class."

"I did," Jenny agreed.

"Come on, then. I know a good place to get a corned-beef sandwich."

Matt gathered up the rope between them as though he were a cowboy collecting his lariat. By tacit agreement he'd become the keeper of the extra length of rope when they traveled from one place to another. Still, they had to leave a foot or so of slack between them so they wouldn't accidentally run into one another when they walked, and with the crowds on the street they occasionally had to stop and wait for someone coming from the other direction to realize they were tied together. Despite that problem, so far they'd remained fairly inconspicuous. But then, it was necessary to do something pretty spectacular to get noticed in New York.

Matt took Jenny to a small Jewish deli, where the corned beef was as good as he'd promised, and unbelievably inexpensive. When they'd nearly finished eating, Jenny reached for the check, only to have

Matt intercept it. She bristled for a moment until he said, "Your half of the tab is $6.87." He stared at her for another moment, a smile lurking at the corners of his mouth. "Does that sound satisfactory to you, *Ms*. Smith?"

Jenny laughed and forked over seven dollars. "Touché! Although, by rights I ought to pay the whole bill, since you wouldn't be here right now if it weren't for my project."

Matt grinned, pleased by the delight he saw on her face. She was downright beautiful when she smiled, and the sound of her laughter made him feel good inside. He realized he was looking forward eagerly to the days ahead, especially the challenge of getting her into his bed. "I'd have to eat even if I were still working full-time," he said as he added money to cover his half of the check. "I feel as if I'm playing hooky from school. What's up this afternoon?"

Matt watched Jenny's throat work as she drained the last of her soda. He wanted to put his mouth on her skin so badly that he could almost taste it already.

"I haven't really got anything planned," Jenny admitted. "I guess I thought we'd play things by ear this first day, just feel things out."

"It's *not* feeling that's going to be the problem,"

Matt countered with a wry smile. As Jenny wrinkled her nose at his comment, he said, "I haven't been to see a movie in the afternoon in years. How does that sound to you?"

"Fine. Let's go see that comedy with—"

"Uh-uh. I'm in the mood for some action and adventure. How about that new cop—"

"Blood and gore? No way," Jenny protested.

"What about that sci-fi—"

"I *hate* sci-fi! I vote for a romance. There's a new French film—"

"You're not actually going to suggest that the two of us sit in a dark theatre and watch some man and woman breathing heavily at one another all afternoon!"

Jenny said nothing.

Matt exhaled noisily. "I see you have exactly that in mind. Does that seem wise to you? I mean, under the circumstances?"

"It's a good test of my theory," Jenny offered. "After all, I want to prove that a man and woman can be more to one another than prospective sexual partners. Just because we watch a romance on the screen doesn't mean we have to project ourselves into the same situation."

"It sounds to me like a test of my willpower," Matt muttered.

Jenny chuckled. "Come on now. You don't really believe either one of us is going to fall all over the other one just because we watch some man and woman making love in a movie, do you?"

Matt thought exactly that. He contented himself with saying, "I think you're making a mistake, but this is your project. If a romantic French movie is all we can agree on, it's better than nothing. Lead the way."

The movie was a mistake. Jenny knew it as soon as the lights went down and the first bare flesh appeared on the screen. She and Matt had separated themselves by a chair, just so they wouldn't accidentally brush elbows or knees in the darkness of the theatre. But Jenny was one of those people who used the movies the way they were intended. She completely lost herself in the fantasy presented on the big screen. So when the dark-haired, blue-eyed Frenchman caressed the woman, Jenny felt his gentle, callused fingertips on her skin. When his lips hovered over the woman's, Jenny felt the tightening deep within her that signaled the beginnings of desire. Her tongue came out to moisten her lips in unconscious preparation for the coming kiss.

When Matt saw Jenny lick her lips he was ready to get up and walk out. But then it would have been obvious that *he* was suffering from sexual arousal, and he'd be damned if he'd give her the satisfaction of seeing him in that condition. But he couldn't help wondering... Did Jenny imagine him as the man on the screen? Did she imagine what it would be like to lie naked under him? He indulged his fantasies, worsening his discomfort.

Jenny's attention was glued to the screen. It wasn't just a man and a woman up there. It was Matt and Jenny. She closed her eyes, her heart pounding furiously, her breathing raspy. My God! What was wrong with her? Matt was a *person*, not a sexual object. How could she be *using* him this way. He'd be furious if he knew....

No he wouldn't Jenny. He'd be pleased.

So you say.

He'd say a man and a woman were created to be together like this. So why fight it?

Who says I'm fighting it?

Then open your eyes.

I can't.

Why not? You're not a coward, are you, Jenny?

Jenny opened her eyes. The woman's face filled the screen, and Jenny knew from the beatific expression that the man was making love to her, making them one. The scene faded, and the man's face came on the screen. Jenny saw Matt's face. Saw the perspiration dotting his upper lip, saw the agonized lines of pleasure on his brow, saw the hooded lids fall over sensually dilated eyes. My God! It was happening again!

Jenny jumped up and yanked on the rope. "Let's go!"

Matt had risen, but he definitely wasn't willing to leave the concealing darkness of the theatre right now. "What's the matter?" he whispered.

"Down in front!" an angry voice shouted.

Jenny's knees were shaking so badly that it didn't take much effort for her to drop back into her chair. Once there, she slumped down as far as she could get. How humiliating! She closed her eyes, crossed her arms and legs, and waited for the movie to end.

Even though she couldn't see, Jenny could still hear the sighs, the whispered words of love.

Finally she leaned across the empty chair and snapped at Matt. "We have to leave! Now!"

She looked wild-eyed, desperate. He had no trouble at all picturing her with her blond hair spread across a pillow, with her chest heaving under him.

"Let's go!" she snapped.

Matt lurched to his feet and pulled Jenny after him out into the sunlight. The two of them blinked owlishly and staggered a little drunkenly as the dizziness of leaving the cold dark theater for the warm outside world quickly passed.

"Where to now, *Ms.* Smith?" Matt demanded.

He was angry. She'd known he would be, but she could deal with his anger better than... She took a deep cleansing breath. "I know a place where we can make a quick stop for coffee and a coffeepot. Then I'd like to go home because I need...I want..."

"Want what?" he prodded.

"Don't rush me. I'm thinking."

She realized that what she really wanted was a little time alone to compose herself. She looked at the silky white cord that hung slack between them and sighed. She wasn't going to get her wish. Wherever she went, he would have to follow.

She glanced at her watch. Not even eight hours together and she was already fantasizing about being in bed with the man. She was distressed by her reaction, because she'd honestly believed the premise she'd set out to prove. The sexes *could* appreciate one another on more than one level. Yes, they were different; she wasn't trying to deny that. But they each had something valuable to offer the other. She just couldn't understand what it was about Matt Benson that made her so vulnerable to him as a man.

Matt's arms crossed forcefully. "Have you made up your mind, *Ms.* Smith?"

Nature gave Jenny some help. There was only one bathroom she knew with a notch in the door to accommodate the rope between them. "Let's get your blasted coffee and go home."

When they arrived at her apartment, Jenny did everything she could think of to avoid the inevitable trip to the bathroom. Finally, she couldn't wait any longer. She'd known it would be embarrassing not to have any privacy; she just hadn't known how embarrassing. It reminded her of the day after her wedding, when she'd seen her family for the first time. They'd known what she'd been doing with Sam all night. It showed in the rosy blush on her face, and in the well-kissed look of her mouth. When she came out of the bathroom in a few minutes she expected to be met by that same knowing glance from Matt.

But when she opened the door she found him lying on the bed closest to the bathroom with his eyes closed. If Jenny hadn't known better, she would have said he was asleep. But of course he wasn't.

"Which bed is yours?" he asked without opening his eyes.

"I'll take the other one, since you seem to have claimed this one."

He opened his eyes and turned lazily onto his side, resting his head on his hand. "I'll be glad to move if you'd rather I had the other bed. I only thought that since you'll probably be using the facilities more than I will, this would be more convenient for both of us."

"That's a rather sexist assumption," Jenny snapped, annoyed because it was also true. When he started to move to the other bed, she stopped him with, "No, wait. I'm sorry. It's all right. I usually sleep in the bed closest to the living room."

Matt paused to stare at her. She was standing with her chin thrust mulishly forward, suggesting that even though she'd just apologized, she'd didn't like the position he'd put her in. Well, that went double for him. "Are you going to analyze everything I say over the next thirty days for its sexist connotation?"

"I told you I'm sorry," Jenny said as she moved to sit cross-legged on the other bed. "Are you sure you're not being deliberately provocative?"

Matt smiled wryly. "Honey, I'm just being myself, but it doesn't seem to take much—"

"Don't call me *honey*," Jenny interrupted.

Matt lay back on the bed and laughed.

"I don't know what you find so funny."

"You," he said between chuckles.

Jenny shook her head in exasperation. "You're the one who's impossible!"

"No, sweetheart, I'm only a man."

Jenny glared. "Sweetheart" wasn't much of an improvement over "honey," and that *man* had to know it.

"Truce?" Matt said, sitting up and holding his open hands out in front of him. "Otherwise it's going to be a long thirty days."

"All right," Jenny reluctantly agreed. "Truce."

"How about you fixing us some supper? I'm getting hungry."

"You know where the kitchen is."

Matt was quiet for a moment. "I'll just wait until you make something. Then I'll have a little of whatever you're having."

Jenny did a slow burn. "Are you sure you'd be willing to eat a simple meal prepared by li'l ole me, darlin'?"

Matt grinned. "You cook it. I'll eat it."

Jenny picked up the phone and called her favorite Chinese takeout. "We can pick it up in a few minutes. Your half comes to $7.92."

Matt pulled out his wallet and threw a ten at her. "By the time you get the table set, the food will be here," he said.

Jenny narrowed her eyes. "*We'll* have the table

set,'' she corrected. ''Whither I goest, thou will go,''
she said, heading for the kitchen.

Matt grimaced as he realized that when she left
the bedroom, he would have to go with her.

Jenny was tired, but what she really wanted was
a little time to herself. She had just reached the living room when the phone rang. She picked up the
extension on the coffee table.

''Hello.'' Jenny listened for a moment before she
said to Matt, ''It's for you. A woman.''

''Oh, that'll be Gertrude Wilson. I gave her your
number.'' Matt plopped down on the couch, and
Jenny headed to the kitchen to set the table.

''Hello, Gerty, are we still on for tomorrow?
Right. I'll pick you up at—'' Matt held his hand
over the phone to ask Jenny, ''Can you be ready to
go out to dinner tomorrow at seven-thirty?''

''We're going to dinner?'' Jenny asked blankly.

''Well, I have a date with Gerty, and, as I recall,
you said this project wasn't going to interfere with
my personal plans. So, can you be ready at seven-
thirty?''

''I guess so. Yes.''

''You there, Gerty? How about if I meet you at
the usual place at eight o'clock? Fine. Bye, honey.
'Til tomorrow. Hmm. I can imagine. Bye.''

Matt's voice had become husky during his farewell, and a slightly lecherous smile lit his face in response to whatever it was Gerty had said that he could "imagine." Jenny didn't need much insight to guess what that might be.

Matt punched the button to end the call and then began dialing again. "I don't suppose a liberated woman like yourself bothers with a sexist activity like dating, so I'll make a reservation for three."

"As a matter of fact," Jenny said, irked to see him so smug about his conclusions, "I do have a date for tomorrow night. We just hadn't made any special plans. So we'll *both* be glad to join you and Gerty for dinner."

"And who might the lucky man be?"

Jenny had to think fast. Who could she call on such short notice to be her date? "Why...it's..." She quickly considered and rejected several men before she said, "Patrick, of course."

Matt frowned, not at all pleased by her announcement. "The photographer?"

"Yes. Patrick the photographer."

"Isn't he a little young for you?"

"How much younger is Gerty than you are?"

"That's beside the point."

"That's *exactly* the point," Jenny argued. "A man reaches his sexual prime in his teens. A woman reaches hers in her thirties. It makes infinitely more sense for an older woman to date a younger man. They're more sexually compatible."

"You don't say."

"It's clear I'm not going to change your mind about this, so why don't we sit down here in the kitchen and—"

Jenny had already headed for her chair when Matt pulled back on the rope that tied them together so that she was stopped and pulled around to face him.

"Don't try to change the subject," Matt said. He was itching to take her in his arms and show her just how sexually compatible with her a man his age could be, but since that wasn't allowed, he contented himself with saying, "Are you saying a man—such as myself—isn't capable of arousing a woman—such as yourself—when he gets past a certain age?"

"Of course I wasn't making such a ridiculous statement," Jenny retorted.

"Then you admit that I'd have no problem arousing you sexually?"

Jenny's eyes widened in disbelief as Matt set down the phone and slipped off the couch, heading for the kitchen, gathering the slack rope between them as he came.

"Just what do you think—"

"Come on. Come to me now," he said, as though speaking to some wild mustang.

Jenny was mesmerized by the desire in his eyes, by the soothing tone of his voice. He tugged her closer and closer until there was no more than an inch or two separating their bodies. She could feel his breath on her face, and they might as well have been touching, since she was so aware of his body heat reaching out to her, of his scent causing her nostrils to flare. It frightened her to realize how much she wanted to reach out and touch him. She stiffened her muscles in an attempt to stop their trembling. How could her body betray her like this?

"Just what are you trying to prove," she asked in an icy voice, "by this little demonstration?"

Matt smiled slightly when he saw the nipples peaking beneath her blouse. She hadn't been unaffected by his nearness, despite what she might want him to believe.

"The premise of this art project is as full of holes as a wormy apple, Jenny. The sexes were never meant to be separate. And as for being equal—well, I've always applauded the differences between a man and a woman. How about you?"

Matt's attack on her project with another of his disgusting food metaphors jolted her to her senses. First it was moldy bread, and now he was comparing her work to wormy apples! Jenny was angry at Matt for taking advantage of the sensual attraction she felt for him, and even more angry with herself for being so foolish as to let down her guard. She slowly backed a few steps away from him before she spoke.

"I don't doubt you've relegated the women you've known to certain limited places in your life—the kitchen and the bedroom," she said, her voice dripping with scorn. "But the point I want to make with this project is that a woman should be more to a man than a cook and a maid and a good time in bed. If you spend a month with me, you'll see that I have the same hopes and desires, the same frustrations and disappointments, as any man. I'm a person, too, Matt."

Jenny's description of him left Matt feeling shallow and callous, and he wasn't very pleased about that. "You make a pretty good case for your project, but it remains to be seen whether your arguments will hold up to scrutiny."

Jenny took a deep breath and said, "Are you going to give this project a chance to succeed?"

"I wasn't aware your success or failure depended on me."

"What I mean is, are you going to sabotage my project by tempting me to touch you again?" Jenny demanded.

To his mortification, Matt blushed. There didn't seem to be a damn thing he could do about it, either.

"I'm sorry if it seemed to you I was purposely playing…" Matt sighed. He *had* been playing games. But what did the woman expect? The whole project struck him as absurd. A Rembrandt superimposed on a Picasso. Nothing fit together.

"I promised not to touch you, Jenny. I can't promise not to try to get you to touch me."

At Jenny's gasp, he admonished, "Before you interrupt, hear me out. I never made any bones about the fact that I don't agree with your point of view. Women and men aren't meant to be separate. They're two parts of a whole. And as for being equal, they aren't. It's as simple as that."

"That's it? Are you finished?"

"I'm finished."

Jenny marched up to Matt and would have poked a finger in his chest if it hadn't meant touching him. She let her voice do the poking instead. "Two parts of a whole? Three-quarters male and one-quarter female, I suppose! However, I agree with your opinion on the lack of equality between the sexes. There isn't a man alive who can measure up to a woman! Stuff that in your pipe and smoke it, macho man!"

"You're beautiful when you're angry."

Jenny stepped away as though she'd been slapped. "Trite, Mr. Benson."

"True, Ms. Smith. Aw, Jenny, this isn't getting

us anywhere. I'm hungry. Let's just take this thing one step at a time. You know where I stand, and you know what you can do about it. I've promised I won't touch you. If you can't keep from touching me, well, that's what this whole project is about, isn't it? If you can't manage to control—"

"You've made your point," Jenny interrupted. "There's no need to discuss this anymore. Let's go pick up the food. I want to finish eating and turn in early tonight. It's been a long day."

Jenny didn't ask for help cleaning up the kitchen after dinner, and Matt didn't offer. Actually, she was too caught up in her thoughts to pay much attention to what was happening around her. She hadn't imagined how stressful it was going to be not to have any respite from Matt's company. For instance, it would have been wonderful, after their argument, to sulk alone in the bedroom. No such luck. She had been forced to endure his cheerful company.

Of even more concern right now, however, was how she was going to get in touch with Patrick about their supposed date. Of course Matt was going to have to use the bathroom sometime, and when he did she could use the phone in the bedroom to call Patrick.

"Are you ready for bed?" Matt asked.

"What? Oh, yes, sure."

"Who's first in the bathroom tonight?" Matt asked.

There it was again, Jenny thought, that enforced discussion of intimate subjects by two people who were practically strangers. "Uh. You can go first, I guess." That would give her a chance to make her call.

Matt led the way to the bedroom. He had his shirt off and was unbuckling his belt when he heard Jenny's hesitant cough.

"Uh...could you do that in the bathroom?"

Matt looked up to find Jenny's gaze locked on the dark curls that covered his chest. "Sure. No problem."

Jenny breathed a sigh of relief as the bathroom door closed behind Matt. In another minute she would have completely embarrassed herself, ogling him like that. She shook her head to clear it of any lingering effects of Matt's physique and reached for the phone, punching out Patrick's number.

It was busy.

She heard the shower go on and imagined Matt stripped down. *Okay, let's think of something else, Jenny girl.* She dialed Patrick again and breathed easier when the phone started ringing.

"Patrick, this is Jenny Smith."

"Hi, Jenny. This is a surprise. What's up?"

"I need a favor."

"Anything for my favorite professor," Patrick quipped.

"You'd better wait to hear what I want before you agree."

"Shoot."

"I want you to go on a date—for dinner—with me tomorrow night."

There was a stunned silence on the other end of the line.

"Patrick? Are you there?"

"I'm here."

Silence again.

"Patrick, I'll understand if you have something else—"

"No." A quick gulp. "No, I'd enjoy going to dinner. You just surprised me. I didn't think you dated."

"I don't."

"Oh."

Jenny heard the shower being turned off and knew she didn't have much time. "I can't explain now, Patrick. Please, I just need you to show up here tomorrow night at seven-thirty as though we've had this date for a while. Can you do that for me?"

"Sure. But why—"

The bathroom door started to open.

"Goodbye, Patrick," Jenny whispered as she settled the phone softly in its cradle.

Steam rolled out as soon as the bathroom door opened, and Jenny was confronted by the sight of Matt with one of her fluffy yellow towels slung around his hips.

"No ventilation," Matt said by way of explanation. "Figured I'd better open the door."

"I've been meaning to get that fan fixed."

"Maybe I can do it while I'm here."

Jenny wasn't paying much attention to the conversation and heard herself reply, "Sure. Anything you say." He had a lovely navel, and she could hardly take her eyes off the line of dark curls that disappeared under the yellow towel. His hair was wet, and water dripped down the back of his neck and over his forehead. He yanked another towel off the rack and used it to blot the soaked rope around his waist.

"Can you help me with this? Do the back?"

Jenny walked toward him like someone in a trance. She took the towel from him and blotted the rope at his back, being careful not to touch him herself. She could feel the play of his muscles under the towel and knew she'd better finish up quick. "If this wet rope gets uncomfortable, you can use the hair dryer—''

"It's no bother. Don't worry about it."

She couldn't help swiping up the droplets of water that had caught along the crease in his back and then worked her way all the way up to his shoulders. "There."

"Thanks." He took the towel from her and slung it around his neck, wiping the streaming water on his face as he carefully squeezed past her and out of the bathroom. "Your turn."

Jenny closed the door after him without quite realizing what she was doing. She turned to lean her back against the wood and looked down at her hands. They were trembling. Her gaze slipped to the bathroom floor, and she almost laughed out loud at what she found.

At the top of a small pile of dirty clothes was the first pair of what she suspected would soon be a tidy heap of Matt's undershorts.

After her shower Jenny blotted the rope as Matt had and realized he was right. The dampness at her waist was noticeable, but not uncomfortable. She wrapped herself in two towels, one above and one below the rope, so she looked like some kind of Polynesian dancer when she opened the bathroom door. When she came out, Matt was already in bed.

He was sitting up reading, and the sheet had settled at his waist. His broad chest was a mass of dark curls, with his nipples peaking out between them. She wanted to feel her fingers in those curls, wanted to feel her hands on his skin. What had she been thinking of when she'd conceived this project? Certainly not this sensual torture.

"Aren't you going to wear some pajamas?" she asked.

"Don't own any."

"Oh." She gave him a sidelong look. Surely he was wearing *something* under that sheet.

"How about you? Going to sleep in those towels?"

"I usually sleep in a T-shirt. I...I didn't have one with me so I—"

"Go ahead and put it on. I won't look," he said with a grin.

Jenny pursed her lips wryly. "Sure..."

True to his word, however, Matt quickly lost himself in his book, and Jenny took her T-shirt and some clean bikini underwear behind the screen she'd put in the corner of the bedroom in anticipation of just such an occasion.

From the corner of his eye Matt saw both towels come to rest on top of the screen. She would be naked now. He liked the way her blond hair fell to her shoulders. She shouldn't keep it tied up on her head the way she did. He wanted to thrust his hands through it and pull her head back for his kiss. He had a vivid imagination, and heat rose in his loins. He raised his knees to hide the evidence of his arousal. Damn. What had he gotten himself into?

Jenny was self-conscious when she came out from behind the screen. She was fully dressed, but from the look Matt was giving her, she might as well have been naked.

Matt didn't mean to stare at Jenny, but he couldn't help himself. Her breasts were high and full under the T-shirt, which was thick enough so that he couldn't see the detail of her nipples. She'd tucked her T-shirt in under the rope, and it came far enough down her thighs that he wanted to slip his hand up underneath. He'd caught a glimpse of her bikini panties when she'd pulled them out of her drawer. He knew they were thin enough so that she'd feel his breath if he kissed her through the silky material.

Abruptly Matt threw his book down on the table between the two beds and turned over on his side, facing away from Jenny.

"Are you going to sleep already?" Jenny asked. It was barely ten-thirty.

"I usually get up early," he grunted. "When are you going to turn out the light?"

"Soon," Jenny promised. "I just want to read a little. It helps me wind down."

Matt closed his eyes, but an hour later he could still feel the glare from the light on his lids. It dawned on him that he hadn't smoked his evening cigarette. No wonder he was so jumpy. Abruptly, he sat up, startling Jenny.

"What's the matter?" she asked.

"I can't sleep with that light on. You're going to have to turn it off," he grumbled.

Jenny stared at the broad, hairy chest, at the tousled hair, the lazy, bedroom eyes. "I always read at least until one," she protested.

"Not for the next thirty days, you don't."

Jenny didn't want to argue with him. If she argued with him, he might stand up, and then... What if he wasn't wearing anything? "All right. Turn over and go back to sleep. As soon as I finish this chap—"

"Now."

When he reached for the sheet that covered him, Jenny acknowledged she had a tiger by the tail. They could argue this out in the light of day. She marked her place, set the book calmly on the nightstand and reached over to turn out the light, plunging the room into darkness. She heard the sheets rustle as he settled back in bed. As quietly as she could, she settled herself as well.

"Jenny…"

"Yes?"

"You look beautiful in bed."

"Trite, Mr. Benson."

"True, Ms. Smith."

It took all Jenny's willpower to turn away from him. He was a man who made her feel like a woman. How was she going to last thirty days without touching him?

Four

Jenny hadn't imagined things could deteriorate so badly overnight, but they had.

How had she managed to pick such a restless sleeper as Matt to partner her on this project? It wouldn't have been so bad that he tossed and turned in his sleep, except that he kept turning in the same direction, gradually winding the rope around his waist. By the middle of the night the rope between them had been pulled taut enough that Matt's next turn had jerked Jenny completely out of bed. She'd landed on the floor with a cry, startling Matt awake.

"What the hell?"

"Look what you've done!" Jenny accused when she finally had the light on. The rope tangled around Matt's waist bore mute testimony to what had happened.

When Matt had stood to untangle the rope, Jenny had gasped and closed her eyes. He hadn't been naked, but with that single glimpse, she'd gotten a pretty good impression of every wonderful masculine thing his trim navy briefs had done little to conceal.

He'd sworn under his breath as he untangled himself. "Are you all right? You're not hurt?"

"I'm fine," Jenny had said breathlessly. With her eyes still closed, she'd felt her way back into bed and turned away from Matt. "Get the light, will you?"

It seemed she'd barely gotten back to sleep when she felt another tug at her waist. Still half asleep, she reached down to see what was causing the problem. She'd forgotten about the rope. Something was jerking at it.

Jenny turned over and lifted her head. The clock showed 5:00 a.m. Matt was on the floor at the foot of their beds, and he was doing sit-ups. She watched his rippling muscles in awe as he changed from sit-ups to push-ups. "What are you doing up at this hour?" she croaked.

"I always exercise in the morning. Keeps me in shape."

"Oh my God," she moaned. She noticed he wasn't breathing hard, even though there was a fine sheen of perspiration on his well-conditioned body. From the waist down he was hidden from her by the other bed. Thank goodness.

Jenny had barely gotten back to sleep when she heard a husky whisper in her ear. "Do you suppose you could slip into my bed so I could take a shower?"

Jenny groaned. "Anything. Just let me sleep. Please."

Jenny didn't even open her eyes; she just groped her way into the other bed. She hadn't been in Matt's bed for more than a minute when a frown furrowed her forehead. She sniffed at the feather pillow she held snuggled in her arms. It smelled like Matthew Benson and some kind of masculine cologne. It was almost as though she held *him* in her arms. Except the pillow was soft, and she imagined Matt would be hard. She sniffed again, then jerked her head upright as the faint scent of Matt's cologne brought home to her exactly where she was and what she was doing. *She was sleeping in Matthew Benson's bed.*

It was 5:45 a.m., and Jenny was suddenly wide

awake. Well, she thought wryly, at least she was no longer *sleeping* in Matthew Benson's bed. She could hear Matt singing in the shower—a popular Broadway tune—and he wasn't a half-bad baritone. How was she going to survive the next twenty-nine days of this insanity?

By 6:00 a.m. Matt was out of the shower. He wanted her to make him some coffee. Jenny wanted to sleep.

"Come on, Jenny. You went to bed half an hour earlier than usual last night. A cup of coffee will get you going."

Jenny opened one bleary eye and announced, "I don't drink coffee."

"Then you can make yourself some tea." Matt started pulling the sheet down, and Jenny grabbed at it.

"All right," she mumbled. "Just let me go to the bathroom. If you don't mind?"

Matt grinned. "I don't mind at all."

The T-shirt had ridden up on Jenny's hips, and Matt was treated to the sight of silky underwear stretched over a cute feminine derriere.

As Matt's grin broadened, Jenny realized what he was gawking at. After a quick look down she gasped and bolted out of bed as if she'd been stung. She took time to wash her face, brush her teeth and slip in her contact lenses, then padded after Matt into the kitchen.

"This is an inhuman time to be awake," she said.

"You miss the best part of the day if you're not up to see the sunrise."

"Thanks, but no thanks."

Matt put some coffee on to perk in the coffee maker they'd bought on the way back from the theater, then turned the burner on under the kettle of water Jenny had left there the previous night. "Don't say I never did you any favors. Now, what are you going to make us for breakfast?"

"I don't want any breakfast. I want to go back to bed."

"Pancakes sound good to me. Here, I'll help. I'll get the mix down from the cupboard for you."

She had to admit the pancakes were good. But she spent most of breakfast blinking her right eye to try to focus it. Her *eyes* knew it wasn't time to get up yet. Her right contact lens was so blurry that she was having trouble seeing, and she was seriously considering taking the darn things out and putting on her glasses. She was vain enough to keep blinking, though, hoping the lens would clear.

She slept unashamedly with her head in her arms while Matt put the dishes in the dishwasher and had a second cup of coffee. When she felt the tug at her waist she rose like a zombie and followed him back into the bedroom. She lay down on Matt's bed again while he headed into the bathroom.

"Where is the damn thing!"

At Matt's furious exclamation, Jenny sat up in bed and asked, "Where's what?"

Matt pulled the bathroom door open and said, "I've lost one of my contact lenses. I thought I put them both in the case last night, but I must have dropped one."

Jenny took turns with Matt searching the bathroom floor, but without any luck.

"We're going to have to go by my optometrist's office and pick up another one before tonight," he said, his mouth grim.

To Jenny's way of thinking, the tortoise-shell glasses he'd put on did nothing to make him look any less attractive. But Matt remained adamant about needing a new lens before his date with Gerty.

"Oh," she teased. "Girls never make passes at guys who wear glasses, huh?"

Matt wasn't amused.

He still needed to shave, she needed to put on her makeup, and there was only one bathroom. They flipped a coin to see who would go first. It didn't help Matt's temper when he lost.

"I'll be out as quickly as I can," Jenny promised.

She kept winking and blinking the whole time she was putting on her makeup, but her right contact didn't get any clearer. With a sigh, she took it out and opened the right side of her lens case to put it away.

But there was already a contact lens in the right side of her case.

Jenny opened the bathroom door. "Matt?"

"What is it, Jenny?" he asked from his sitting position at the head of the bed.

"I...uh...I found your contact lens."

He was standing beside her in an instant. "Hey! Really? That's great. Where was it?"

Jenny gulped and replied, "In my eye."

"What?"

"I...uh...I must not have been paying attention when I put my lenses in this morning. It seems I put in my left lens and your right one. The cases were both on the sink and..."

She'd expected Matt to be furious. Instead he threw back his head and laughed. "I can't believe it! You never noticed the difference?"

"It looks just like mine!" Jenny protested. "And it didn't feel uncomfortable, it only looked blurry."

"I guess your eyesight must be a little worse than mine," Matt said with a grin.

"I guess so," Jenny agreed. She couldn't help

smiling back at him. He was awfully attractive when he smiled.

"Hurry up and finish," Matt urged. "I've got thirty minutes of walking to do before I get started today."

Jenny just gaped. "Say that again."

"What?"

"That part about the thirty minutes of walking."

Matt looked sheepish as he admitted, "I usually run in the mornings, as well as do exercises. I realized that wouldn't be possible this month, so I thought I'd compromise with a brisk walk."

"I do enough walking in New York without volunteering to do more."

"Come on, Jenny," Matt coaxed. "It'll be good for you. Get your heart pumping."

Matt was close enough that Jenny's heart was doing a fine job of pumping without the need for a thirty-minute walk.

"Please, Jenny?"

He was like a little boy asking for the other half of her popsicle, and Jenny had always been a sucker for sad eyes and a pout. "All right. But you'll keep your pace matched to mine, not the other way around."

"Agreed. If we walk for half an hour, we'll be

just in time to meet Mark Zimmerman at his gallery when it opens,'' Matt said.

Jenny stood up in surprise. ''But I have to work this morning. I thought you'd be coming with me.''

''You said you only taught Tuesdays and Thursdays.''

''I do. But I also told you that I have another source of income. I spend the rest of the week at my studio,'' Jenny explained.

''What studio?''

''It's a loft over a boutique in SoHo. I work there with a friend of mine.''

He wondered whether her friend was male or female, but he would be damned before he'd admit to himself it mattered. ''What do you do? I thought your specialty was performance art.''

''It is, but I have to earn a living, too.''

Matt didn't look convinced. ''What kind of art earns you a decent living?''

''I make wearable art for the boutique downstairs from the studio.''

Jenny sat down cross-legged on Matt's bed while he headed into the bathroom. It was an intimate thing to watch a man shave, Jenny thought. She ignored the tensing in the pit of her stomach as he slathered lather over his cheeks, chin and throat.

He took the first swipe with his razor, and while

he was rinsing it under the running water in the sink said, "I've heard about wearable art, but I haven't paid much attention to it. Do you enjoy your work?"

"I love it. I use a mixture of unlikely fabrics, add leather, lace, baubles, a variety of trims—everything from dried pasta to drapery cord—and create something to wear that's unique enough to be called art. I also do accessories—hats, purses, shoes and jewelry."

"And women pay good money for that sort of thing?"

Jenny shrugged to disguise her shiver as Matt stroked the razor from his Adam's apple up to his chin. "The few who can afford it."

"What you make is that expensive?"

"They're buying a piece of art, a piece of an artist's heart and soul. It doesn't come cheap." Jenny swallowed as Matt finished shaving and rinsed off the last of the lather, leaving the angled planes of his face bare to her gaze. She'd wondered how he shaved those long grooves on either side of his mouth. She almost giggled out loud as she thought, Very carefully!

Matt turned to look at Jenny. He'd been aware that her eyes hadn't left him the whole time he'd shaved. Hell, he'd almost nicked himself twice trying to get the whole business over with before his trembling hand cut his throat. Then he'd caught sight of the wooden plaque in the corner of the bathroom. When he'd read it, he'd actually drawn blood.

Bigamy is having one husband too many.
    Monogamy is the same thing.

It reminded him again of their differences. How could a woman—especially this one—affect him this way?

Somehow, even though she'd been watching him, he'd managed to listen to what she had to say about her wearable art. The way she'd explained it, a simple skirt and blouse were elevated to the stature of a Rembrandt. He was intrigued enough to want to see some of her work.

Just as Matt sneaked a peek at her, Jenny looked at her watch and exclaimed, "I can't believe this. It's only 8:00 a.m.!"

"How did you get so bound to your wristwatch?" Matt let the irritation he felt at his attraction to her come through in his voice.

"I'm not—"

"You looked at your watch twelve times last night. I counted." He hadn't, but how could she know that? "And God knows how many times you've checked the time this morning."

"Thanks to you, I certainly got an early start," Jenny replied in an acerbic tone. "I like to know what time it is. What's wrong with that?"

"Nothing, I suppose. But it makes you different from most of the other artists I know."

"How so?"

"You can't be unfettered and independent, spontaneous, if you will, when you're watching a clock. Being time-bound takes away the freedom to do things whenever you feel like it."

Jenny shook her head in disbelief. "How do you manage to get where you need to be on time?"

"Sometimes I'm late," Matt admitted with a grin. "But if I am, it's because I haven't let a clock stop me when I was having a good time doing something else."

"That sounds more like irresponsibility than freedom to me," Jenny countered.

"Want to try it for a day—as an experiment, like this project?"

Jenny's eyes narrowed suspiciously. "What would I have to do?"

"First, take off your watch."

After a moment of thought, she complied.

"Now, don't think about what time it is for the rest of the day."

Jenny's lips pursed while she waged an inner battle. "To be honest, I'm not sure I can do that," she admitted.

"I didn't think I could spend thirty days tied to a beautiful woman without touching her, either, but I'm managing. Where's your sense of adventure?"

Jenny didn't know whether to be flattered that he thought her beautiful or furious that he'd agreed to be her partner when he had such reservations. At any rate, his challenge spurred her to say, "All right. You're on. Are there any stakes in this game?"

"What did you have in mind?"

"Since you're aiming to break one of my habits, it seems only fair for me to get a shot at breaking one of yours."

Matt had a sinking feeling he knew what was coming. She didn't disappoint him.

"If I manage to make it through the day without asking about the time, you'll go a day without any cigarettes."

"And if you don't make it?" he asked.

"Then I'll take down my No Smoking signs and bring in an ashtray so you can have your evening cigarette in bed."

That sounded great to Matt, and he was pretty sure she wouldn't last long without needing to know the time, so with a smile and a wink, he agreed. "Now, are you ready for that walk?"

Jenny fought the urge to look at her watch. "Whenever you are. Where are we going after our walk? I do have to work, Matt. It's how I pay the rent."

"How about a compromise?" he suggested. "Let me spend an hour or so checking out this artist's work, then I'll come with you to your studio. I can write up my reactions while you're working. How does that sound?"

"Fine, except how will I know when your hour is up?"

Matt laughed. "You can count the seconds under your breath if it'll make you feel any better."

"I just might," Jenny muttered. "Are you ready to go?"

"I need to put in my newfound lens."

Jenny fought a blush of embarrassment. "Sure. I'll wait."

When they walked out the front door of her apartment, Jenny unconsciously looked at her wrist to see what time it was.

Matt smirked.

Jenny grimaced back at him. "Let's go. We'll be—" Jenny bit her tongue to keep from making a reference to how late they'd be if they didn't hurry.

There was one good thing about Matt's challenge. Jenny was so busy worrying about what time it was

that she completely forgot about the fact that they
were tied together. The whole time they walked, her
mind was concentrated on whether they'd be late for
Matt's appointment. Not that she cared, of course.
If he wanted to spend his whole life missing the
party, who was she to suggest he do otherwise?

Jenny couldn't help wondering, though, what it
would be like to live with someone who was so
cavalier about time. She'd learned her lesson the
hard way. Life was to be lived every minute. You
never knew when the fates were going to step in and
steal it away. Jenny kept track of time because she
knew it was not an unlimited commodity. Without
her watch she felt reckless, as though she were daring the powers that be to rob her while she wasn't
paying attention.

"You're quiet," Matt observed when they were
nearly at their destination.

"I was thinking."

"Mmm."

Jenny eyed Matt, wondering how to explain her
obsession with the clock. Before she could come up
with anything, he said, "Here we are."

The SoHo gallery was no different than a dozen
others Jenny had visited. It consisted of a rectan-
gular room with a high ceiling, neutral-colored
walls, track lighting, and polished wooden floors,

with a few paintings and sculptures tastefully hung
or situated at precise intervals.

The gallery owner also reminded Jenny of a
dozen others she'd met. He took one look at her and
saw a woman, not an artist. It wasn't the first time
it had happened, and it wouldn't be the last.

The two men greeted one another, shook hands
cordially, and then Matt turned to introduce Jenny.

"Jenny, I want you to meet Mark Zimmerman.
He owns this gallery. Mark, this is Jenny Smith."

Mark extended his hand to Jenny, and when she
reached out to take it, covered it with his own. He
used that grip to pull Jenny closer, invading her
space until they were uncomfortably close. "Jenny.
How lovely you are. Why haven't we met?"

"I've never been here before," Jenny said flatly.

Matt had seen lines delivered more smoothly, but
it wasn't Mark's line that bothered him. It was the
fact that it had been delivered to Jenny. Did Mark
think he'd brought Jenny here just so Mark could
make a move on her? He'd soon disabuse Mark of
that notion. "Jenny's an artist," Matt found himself
saying.

"Oh, really?" Mark replied dismissively. He
started to lead Jenny away from Matt, saying,
"Well, while you're busy out here, I have some

paintings in the back that Jenny might enjoy see-ing.''

On her next step the rope that bound Jenny to Matt pulled her up short. "Uh, excuse me," she said.

Mark turned, a concerned frown marring his fore-head while he tried to figure out what had happened.

"Jenny's staying with me," Matt said.

"Why? There's no reason why she can't—"

Matt held up the rope that bound them and pulled up the extra line until Jenny was standing beside him again. "Sorry, old man. Jenny and I have tied the knot."

"Yes. Well." Mark was clearly flustered and not a little confused. "I didn't know… I hadn't heard… Well, I'll leave the two of you alone, then. Call me if you need me."

Matt didn't wait for Mark to disappear from the room before he began to chuckle.

"I suppose you thought that little scene was funny," Jenny said.

"Did you see the look on his face?"

"Sure. It was the look of one male animal re-sponding to another who'd invaded his territory," Jenny replied tartly.

Matt pulled Jenny a little closer, so there wasn't more than an inch between them. "You bet. No man's ever poached on my territory and gotten away with it.''

The rumbling voice in her ear left Jenny weak-kneed, so she was a little late in protesting Matt's possessiveness. ''Of all the idiotic—''

He stepped back abruptly and said, ''Of course, I have no claim at all on you, Jenny. We're only together to prove my point.''

''Which is?''

''Women are women. Men are men.''

''Aaaargh!''

''I'd better get busy,'' Matt said. With that he turned and began an intense study of the several paintings Mark had asked him to come here to see.

While Matt examined the paintings, Jenny searched surreptitiously for a clock and was frustrated beyond belief when there was none to be found. She moved to the end of her tether, hoping that the farther away from Matt she was, the easier it would be to think. It was clear that the past twenty-four hours hadn't moved him off ground zero. Hadn't he recognized the discrimination in Mark's attentions to her? How would he like to be treated strictly as a sexual object? One of the reasons so few women artists got shown in galleries like this was because first they had to get past the Mark Zimmermans of the world.

Jenny had no idea how much time had passed, but she saw that Matt had stepped away from the paintings and was now viewing them as a whole, rather than individually.

"What do you think of them?" Jenny asked.

"They're a perfect example of what happens when an untrained individual tries to create art."

"Then you don't like them."

"I didn't say that. In fact, if I were only looking at this painting—" Matt pointed to large canvas of a woman seated at a dressing table. "—I'd say the artist shows promise."

"Then what did you mean—"

"This particular painting appeals to me. But the rest of these…" Matt gestured to the other canvases displayed for his perusal. "…prove that this painting was a fluke, a stroke of luck. No, this lady should have—"

"These paintings are by a woman artist?"

"Can't you tell?"

"No. Can you?"

"Of course."

Jenny stared at Matt in awe. "You're either lying or kidding. I can't decide which."

Matt laughed. "In this case it was easy," he explained. "Artists are like writers. They paint what they know, what they feel. See this background? A woman's vanity, all these knickknacks. That's a woman's subject matter.''

''Of all the sexist things I've ever heard you say, I think this is the worst,'' Jenny railed. ''I suppose if the paintings had been of race cars you would have said they were by a man.''

''They probably would be.''

Jenny turned away from Matt and spied an abstract piece of art done in aluminum. She pointed and said, ''All right, smarty-pants. Was that piece created by a male or female artist?''

''Male. Those two lumps are obviously breasts, and those two long skinny rods are legs. I'd bet money that piece is a labor of love created by a man.''

Jenny stared in amazement at the twisted aluminum. In the first place, that Matt could see a woman in the thing at all was phenomenal. In the second place, she knew at least two women who spent hours drawing female figures. In the third place...he had to be bluffing.

Jenny snickered. ''All right, hotshot. Let's get Mark in here to give us the names of these artists.''

Jenny spent the whole trip from the SoHo gallery to her loft workshop muttering to herself. The woman before the vanity had been painted by a woman. The twisted aluminum sculpture had been created by a man. How had Matt known? Jenny found the whole situation totally disgusting. It seemed that Matt was doing a much better job of convincing her of the differences between the sexes than she was of convincing him that the sexes were equal.

Jenny was eager to reach her workshop. She hadn't realized precisely why until she saw the clock across from her worktable. She would be able to sneak a peek at the time without having to ask about it.

Matt was on the lookout for a clock, and sure enough he saw it. He stepped ahead of Jenny and turned the clock face toward the wall.

"What did you do that for?" she demanded.

"Wouldn't want you to be tempted to cheat," he said with a grin.

Jenny glowered. But not for long. Her partner wasn't someone who could be ignored, and he promptly introduced himself to Matt, extending a large hand as he did so.

"I'm Jason Martin."

The man in front of him didn't fit Matt's image of the typical male fashion designer—even if what he designed was wearable art. He was the size of a linebacker for the New York Jets, with a grip to match. On the other hand, the smile on his face was openly friendly, disarming, even charming.

"Not what you expected, huh?" Jason asked.

Matt was startled that Jason not only recognized his surprise but acknowledged it. He smiled ruefully. "I have to admit I expected someone a little less..."

"Large?" Jason asked, returning the grin.

Here was another man in Jenny's life that Matt found hard not to like. He wondered if their business relationship had ever extended into the bedroom, but there was nothing in the easy camaraderie between the two of them to give him the answer one way or the other.

"Jason and I have been working together for four years now," Jenny said. "We know each other well enough to survive each other's moods."

The look that passed between Jenny and Jason wasn't the least bit reassuring to Matt. If they hadn't been lovers, they nonetheless possessed a closeness he envied.

"You're late," Jason said to Jenny.

Even though there was no censure in Jason's voice, Matt said promptly, "I'm responsible for that. I had to go by a gallery this morning to view some artwork."

"I just placed you. You're the critic for *Artist's World*, aren't you?" All the pleasantness had gone out of Jason's voice. "The one who panned Jenny's work."

"I am." Matt thought that, if possible, Jason had somehow gotten larger, something like the effect of ruffled plumage on a riled fighting cock.

"I suppose you didn't agree with my review, either," Matt said, carefully holding his ground in the face of Jason's challenging stance.

"No, I didn't," Jason admitted. He turned to Jenny and said, "I thought I'd talked you out of using this guy for your next project. What changed your mind?"

"I hoped that if Matt followed me around for thirty days, he'd see what I'm trying to do," Jenny replied.

"And you expected him to be open-minded enough to really admit that he was wrong?"

"I am that open-minded," Matt inserted, once more drawing Jason's attention. Matt met the other man's steady gaze until Jason turned his back on him and said to Jenny, "We have an entire outfit to finish this afternoon, complete with purse, hat and shoes."

Jenny was already rolling up her sleeves. "What ti—" Jenny cut herself off just as she was about to ask the time and shot a quick look at Matt. Fortunately he wasn't paying attention, apparently distracted by the huge amounts of paraphernalia they used to create their wearable art.

"We'd better get busy, then," Jenny said to Jason.

It was amazing how fast the afternoon passed. Even without her watch, she could tell from the lengthening shadows through the row of windows that lined one wall of the loft that it was getting late. An even better indication of the passing time was the fatigue in her shoulders. Without her even saying anything, Jason came up behind her and began to massage her aching muscles. Jenny groaned with pleasure.

Matt watched the interplay between Jason and Jenny with consternation. Jason's touch was comforting, the touch of a friend. Matt knew that if he'd been the one massaging Jenny's shoulders it wouldn't have been long before his hands slipped around to touch her breasts. But that was because he thought of Jenny as a woman, he realized, rather than merely as a person. Jason treated her as someone special, but not as a sexual someone.

To the best of his knowledge, Matt had never had a woman friend who remained a friend. Somehow the relationship always seemed to progress beyond that and they became lovers. He could see that the friendship between Jason and Jenny was deep and caring, and that it obviously brought a great deal of satisfaction to both of them. It gave him some food for thought. Perhaps that was what Jenny meant when she argued that she was a person as well as a woman.

Jenny rolled her head slowly. "I'm about ready to call it a day."

"We got everything done but the shoes. I can come in tomorrow and take care of them, if you want to get out of here," Jason said.

"You ready to go, Matt?" Jenny inquired.

Matt had finished his review hours ago, but he'd been so fascinated by the creativity he'd witnessed that he hadn't minded the wait at all. "I guess we'd better get going if we want to make our reservations at the restaurant tonight."

Jenny groaned. "The last thing I want to do is—"

"You aren't anxious to see Patrick?"

Jenny realized at once the mistake she'd made. Actually, Patrick would be good company. But Jenny would have given a lot to be able to curl up in bed with a steamy romance novel tonight instead of heading out on the town. She cursed whatever demons had caused her to lie to Matt about having a date with Patrick. She had no choice now but to make the best of a bad situation. She had absolutely no idea what she was going to do when the time came to give Patrick a good-night kiss.

Five

Matt had never seen anything to compare with the outfit Jenny had on when she emerged from the bathroom. It was as though she had metamorphosed from a caterpillar into a butterfly. Not that he hadn't thought Jenny was beautiful before, but once she donned one of her wearable art creations, she assumed another dimension. Perhaps it was the fact that he was fascinated with what she was wearing, but Matt had trouble taking his eyes off her.

The contrasts of texture between lace and leather, silk and corduroy, the contrasts of color between pink and blue, red and purple, the multiple layers of cloth in the bodice, the trail of pearls across her shoulder and down to the crevice between her breasts, and the tight, thigh-slit sheath that lovingly enfolded her hips, all combined to leave him breathless.

"That's really something," Matt said. "Is that one of your creations?"

"Yes." Jenny didn't have to ask if he liked it. His pleasure at her appearance showed in the warmth of his gray eyes and in the curve of his full lips. They had managed to agree on who would use the bathroom first and where they would dress so they wouldn't trip over one another, but the occasional tug on the rope when Matt moved made Jenny constantly aware of the connection between them.

They were both ready before Patrick came to the door, so they settled in the living room together to wait for him, Jenny in the bamboo chair and Matt on the sofa. Matt was dressed in a crisply starched Oxford cloth shirt that they'd picked up from the laundry on the way back from her workshop, a conservative tie and a pair of dark pleated pants. He'd laid his jacket over the sofa for later.

"I have to admit I'm surprised we finished dressing on time," Jenny said to fill the uncomfortable silence that had grown between them. "I could have sworn we wouldn't make it."

"Goes to show that forgetting about time is one of the best ways of stretching it. How did an artist like you get so obsessed with the clock?"

Matt watched Jenny's features closing and knew before she spoke that she wasn't going to answer him. He was saved from having to confront her by a knock on the front door.

"That'll be Patrick." Jenny wished she'd reminded Patrick not to bring his camera, but was relieved when she opened the door to find him without it. "Patrick, welcome."

Jenny sensed Matt waiting behind her to see how she greeted Patrick. She could see no way out of it. She raised herself on tiptoes and kissed Patrick on the cheek. "I'm so glad to see you."

If Patrick was still confused by her abrupt invitation to come to dinner, Jenny saw no signs of it. In fact, he took full advantage of the situation. Before she could step away from him, he grasped her waist and pulled her close, planting a kiss smack on her lips.

"Patrick!"

"Hello, Jenny," he said with a pleased grin on his face. "Where are we going tonight?"

Matt had kept his doubts to himself about Jenny's "date" with Patrick. But while her greeting might have been satisfactorily tentative, Patrick's wasn't.

Now Matt extended his hand to Patrick. "We meet again. We're headed for Ciro's. It's an Italian place in lower Manhattan. We'll be meeting my friend Gertrude Wilson there at eight o'clock."

"Then I guess we'd better be going." Patrick placed a proprietary hand under Jenny's elbow. "It's nearly that now."

So much for being on time, Jenny thought, sending a wry glance Matt's way. He merely grinned and shrugged.

"Are we taking a cab or the subway?" Patrick asked.

Matt turned to Jenny, and they said together, "Cab."

Jenny's worst nightmare was of the subway door closing with her on the inside and Matt on the outside. She'd made up her mind when she'd decided to do this project that she'd foot the extra expense for a cab when it was necessary to travel farther than walking distance.

Patrick sat between Jenny and Matt in the back seat of the cab, his arm draped around her shoulder. Jenny wished there were some way to get Patrick alone long enough to tell him why she'd asked him out. From his actions she could see that he considered her invitation sincere, and if appearances were any guide, she'd have her hands full fending him off before the evening was done.

Gertrude Wilson, or Gerty, as Matt so irreverently called her, was nothing like Jenny had pictured her based on her sedate, old-fashioned name. What Jenny had expected was someone about Matt's age, attractive, of course, but in a sedate, old-fashioned way. What she found was a stylishly dressed, long-legged, well-endowed woman with big blue eyes and bright red hair in a shade God could never have imagined. She guessed Gerty was a good fifteen years younger than Matt, and Jenny, at thirty, felt old enough to be Gerty's aunt.

Gerty gushed. Not that she wasn't a sweet child, Jenny thought, but she just never shut up. How could Matt stand to be around her? Jenny had her answer when they got up to dance after dinner to the big-band sounds of the restaurant's small orchestra. Gerty's arms went around Matt's neck, her belly fit into his hips, and Jenny was sure you couldn't wedge a toothpick between them.

Of course, when Matt danced with Gerty, Jenny was forced to dance with Patrick. Patrick took his lead from Matt, and before she could protest, she found herself fitted tightly against Patrick's hard body. The only good thing Jenny could see in the situation was that she would be able to whisper in Patrick's ear and explain what was going on.

"Patrick," she breathed.

"Yes, darling. What is it?"

To Jenny's alarm, Patrick was kissing her ear. "Patrick, you have to stop that and listen to me," she said desperately.

"Darling, I can hear you." His lips drifted down to her throat.

"Oh, my God," Jenny groaned. "Patrick, listen. About this date—I had to ask you out. I had no choice." Jenny took a deep breath and rattled off, "Matt was going to see Gerty, and he assumed I never dated, and of course he's right, but I couldn't let him know that, so I said I had a date, and when he asked me with whom I couldn't think of anybody I could ask, but then I remembered you, so I told him I had a date with you, and then I couldn't get away from him to call you and explain everything because he was coming out of the bathroom, and, Patrick, if you don't stop kissing me I'm going to cause you great bodily pain."

Abruptly Patrick lifted his head and stared at Jenny, as though everything had suddenly clicked in his head, "Then you don't have the hots for me?"

"Shhh!" Jenny grabbed Patrick's nape and pulled his head back down so she could whisper in his ear.

"Keep it down. I don't want Matt to hear this. And no, I don't have the hots for you." To the drowned-dog look in Patrick's blue eyes Jenny responded, "I'm sorry, Patrick. You're a good friend and my favorite student. I thought you wouldn't mind helping me out. Was I right?"

Gradually a grin began to grow on Patrick's face. "You were right. Just what hypothesis is it that we're going to prove here tonight, Professor Smith?"

"That I can be both a feminist and a desirable, sensual, sexual woman," Jenny said wryly. "In other words, Patrick, I want you to do exactly what you were doing. I just didn't want you to be hurt when you found out later..."

"I understand," Patrick said quickly. "Sure, Professor Smith. I'm at your service. Let's see. Where was I?" He leaned down and tickled Jenny's ear with his tongue, causing her to laugh.

Matt's head came up at the sound of Jenny's husky laughter. He'd been wrong about her again. There certainly wasn't anything wrong with Jenny's sex appeal. Or Patrick's response to it, he thought ruefully. When she'd first shown up in his office, she'd been a series of contradictions. The buttoned-up blouse, with the cat-clawed sleeves. Slinky black pants that fit her like a glove, but hair twisted tight to her head without a strand out of place. She'd looked like a reference librarian from Cleveland heading for a Friday night disco.

The woman dancing with Patrick was nothing if not fashionable. Her dress was slashed high to show off her long legs, and while no cleavage was actually revealed, the line of pearls drew the eye in that direction. She'd curled her hair—he'd seen it on the rollers—but it wasn't frizzy, just a riot of soft waves that bounced with the sway of her head.

Gerty tilted her hips into Matt's, demanding his attention. "I didn't know we were going to have company tonight, lover."

"As you can see," Matt said, letting the excess rope sway in the hand he held at her back, "I'm going to be tied up for the next few weeks."

Gerty pouted. She did it almost as well as she gushed. "I'd planned to spend the night with you. I suppose that isn't possible now."

"No. I'm afraid not." Much as it pained him, Matt was forced to admit that George's adjective, "addlepated," probably fit Gerty better than it should. He'd never really noticed it before, but the contrast with Jenny's wit and intelligence was striking. When he looked at Gerty as a person, and not just a female, she seemed singularly lacking in appeal.

That was when Matt knew he was in trouble. It wasn't that he minded having his consciousness raised—or whatever they called it—only that he wasn't sure what would happen when he replaced Gerty with a woman like...like Jennifer Smith. She was opinionated, headstrong, stubborn, independent—not bad traits, he had to admit—only he liked his women a little more pliable.

Of course, Jenny was also creative, intelligent, fun to be with and not bad-looking. All right. She was beautiful. So what? What good was beauty if the woman wasn't going to let you near enough to enjoy it? Matt chanced a glance at Jenny and Patrick. On the other hand, Patrick certainly wasn't having any problems getting close.

They dropped Gerty off on the way home, and Jenny tried not to watch as Matt kissed her good-night, because the kiss went on...and on. Just when she thought Matt might turn and come down the steps, Gerty caught him again, and it took a few more minutes for him to get back to them. As he reached the cab, Jenny turned quickly to Patrick and said, "You're going to have to kiss me good-night, Patrick. And you're going to have to make it look good."

Patrick didn't smile. "Are you sure about this, Jenny? If the guy's such a jerk he can't see—"

"Hello again, Matt," Jenny interrupted. "I take it Ms. Wilson didn't want the evening to end just yet."

"You took it right. *Miss* Wilson knows how to make a man feel like a man."

He was angry, but for the life of her, Jenny couldn't figure out why. "Is something wrong, Matt?"

He leaned over and muttered into Jenny's ear, "I'm reduced to double-dating like a high school kid and saying good-night at the door. Yet I'm going home to sleep in the same room with a woman from whom I've promised to keep my distance. And you ask me if something is wrong?"

Thankfully, by then the cab had delivered them to the front stoop of Jenny's apartment, and Matt swung out of the cab and headed for the door. He didn't get far before the rope brought him up short.

"Looks like he doesn't care to wait to see your good-night kiss, Jenny," Patrick remarked quietly.

"He doesn't have much choice," Jenny said.

When they reached the front door, Matt opened it and stepped inside, but he left the door open. "Are you coming?"

"In a moment," Patrick said. He swept Jenny into his arms and kissed her with all the passion he felt for her, which he knew was more than she was willing to allow. If he was only going to have this one chance to let her know his feelings, he was going to take advantage of it.

Jenny threw herself into the kiss and found it surprisingly enjoyable. But she didn't feel that arc of awareness, that frisson of desire, that had come with the mere brush of her fingertips against Matt's belly. She hadn't allowed herself this much involvement with a man in a long time, and she was glad she'd told Patrick ahead of time that their date was a pretense, because she could also tell from the kiss that he felt more for her than she felt for him.

"Thank you, Patrick," she murmured, when he finally broke the kiss. "It was a lovely evening."

"We'll do it again sometime," he promised. Then he was gone.

Jenny was still pensive when she turned and stepped inside her apartment, but to Matt she looked stunned. Her lips were still damp and a little swollen from the force of Patrick's kiss. He'd never wanted anything so much as he wanted to take her into his bed right now.

"I want you, Jenny." He hadn't realized he'd spoken out loud until she turned to him. Her pupils were dilated with desire, and she actually walked a step toward him before she seemed to shake herself awake.

"What am I doing?" she said with a little laugh. "Whew! I must have had one too many glasses of wine this evening. I thought you said—"

"I did."

Jenny swallowed hard. She looked toward the bedroom door, then headed for the kitchen and a cup of tea, even though she was exhausted. The bedroom was no place to be with Matt until she could do something about the tremendous need that had turned her footsteps in his direction the instant he'd called to her. She sought for a distraction. "I thought you wanted Gerty Wilson."

Matt followed her to the kitchen, aware of what she was doing. She was right. The bedroom was no place for them right now. "Gerty's the perfect date—for a male chauvinist pig."

Jenny couldn't help smiling. "You don't say."

"But she's no longer perfect for me."

Jenny arched a questioning brow. "No?"

"At least, not for the next twenty-eight days," he qualified. There was no reason to let her know he was beginning to question his chauvinistic beliefs so soon. She was liable to cut the project short, and Matt had a feeling that the next twenty-eight days were going to be some of the most interesting of his life.

Matt didn't help her make the coffee, even though

she fumbled through it, because it allowed him to watch her. When she finally set a cup in front of him, he sipped it in silence. It was awful, but she could learn to make coffee. He wondered if she could also learn to share herself with him the way she'd shared herself with Patrick tonight. He couldn't remember the last time he'd been jealous of another man. It wasn't a feeling he wanted to cultivate.

Jenny was satisfied with the silence, but she was so tired that in a few moments her eyelids began to droop. "I've got to get some sleep," she said finally. "Are you ready for bed?"

The husky tremor in her voice sent a shiver through Matt. He could last for thirty days. He'd promised her he would. "You're right. It's late. Let's go to bed."

Jenny headed for the bedroom, slipping out of her heels as she went. She let them lie where they fell.

"What? It isn't like the Pristine Princess," Matt mocked, "to leave shoes strewn across the living room."

Jenny turned her head over her shoulder long enough to say, "Stuff it, Matt."

Matt laughed, and suddenly the tension that had kept them prisoner since they'd entered the apartment dissipated. Jenny slipped behind the screen to dress, and while her back was turned Matt stripped down to his briefs, brushed his teeth in the bathroom and then slipped under the sheets.

That was how Jenny found him when she came from behind the screen. "That was quick."

"I've got my contact lens case here by the bed— just so there aren't any more mistakes—and I've brushed my teeth. What else is there?"

Jenny grimaced and padded to the bathroom door, closing it firmly behind her. She could sure use a set of male kidneys. When she'd been pregnant with Sarah she'd spent more time in the bathroom... Tears misted Jenny's eyes at the thought of her daughter. If she'd only known then how little time... The cold water on her face took care of her tears, so by the time she stepped from the bathroom no residue of the painful past remained.

"You left toothpaste in the sink," Jenny admonished as she came out of the bathroom.

Matt yawned. "I'll get it tomorrow morning, along with the laundry on the floor."

Jenny slipped into bed and reached for the book on the table.

"You're not going to read, are you?"

"I was. I guess I won't, if it's going to bother you."

"It's going to bother me." Matt rolled over and

closed his eyes. "Let's turn out the light, Jenny, and get some sleep. It's past two in the morning."

"I win!" Jenny crowed.

"What?"

When Matt opened his eyes enough to see her, she was standing triumphantly on her bed with her arms crossed under her breasts and a huge grin on her face. "I didn't mention the time once today. You're the one who brought it up first."

Matt groaned. "I suppose you want to collect on your bet tomorrow."

"Why not? It'll be good practice. We have to fly to San Francisco tomorrow evening, and I'm not sitting in the smoking section of the plane."

Matt calculated the length of the flight to San Francisco from New York. He could probably make it without a cigarette that long, but he was a nervous flyer, and a cigarette helped. "We'll talk about it tomorrow," he said.

Jenny didn't answer. It was the first time in a long time that she'd enjoyed a day without contemplating the fragility of life. She owed Matt a great debt of gratitude for that. But in order to thank him, she'd have to explain what had bound her to the clock in the first place. And after only two days, Jenny wasn't yet ready to bare her soul. Despite the fact she was living with Matt, despite the fact she liked

him...and desired him...they were still virtual
strangers. She would have to wait and see whether
Matt Benson turned out to be the kind of person she
could confide her deepest thoughts to—the kind of
person with whom she might like to share her life.

Jenny had known sleep wouldn't come easily, but
she'd counted on getting a full eight hours' rest
when it finally did. The tug on her waist at the break
of dawn proved she was wrong. She caught a
glimpse of Matt's shoulders as he was doing his
push-ups. She turned over and hid her face in the
pillow, but she still saw the sweat-dampened flesh.
It seemed like moments later when Matt's husky
voice rasped in her ear, "Would you mind getting
into my bed, Jenny?"

"Don't forget the toothpaste in the sink," she
mumbled as she complied, careful not to open her
eyes.

They spent the day in easy camaraderie, packing
for the trip, picking up the tickets at the travel
agency and catching the flight out in the evening.
Jenny had called ahead to the airport to say that she
and Matt would be tied together with a rope and to
explain the nature of her project. Although there
were a few stares at the security gate, they made it
through with a minimum of fuss.

Things didn't go quite so smoothly once they got

to San Francisco. Jenny had booked reservations at a hotel far enough in advance to make sure they'd have twin beds, but it seemed there had been some mix-up, and the only room left had a single king-size bed. Jenny would just as soon have gone to another hotel, but with the three-hour time difference, it was already midnight in New York, so she was exhausted, and without a reservation they would have a tough time finding other accommodations at nine o'clock on a Saturday night.

When the young man at the registration desk reconfirmed that nothing else was available, Jenny made a decision. "We'll take it."

She breathed a sigh of relief when she saw the bed. It was huge. She glanced surreptitiously at Matt. He wasn't chewing the inside of his cheek anymore. Surely they wouldn't have too much trouble sleeping in such a big bed together and keeping to the restriction of not touching one another. Just in case, she planned to bundle the bedspread between them.

"You can have the bathroom first," Matt said.

"All right." It was then that it dawned on Jenny that the bathroom was considerably farther from the bed than in her apartment. In fact, if she had reason to use the facilities during the night, as she sometimes did, she'd have to wake Matt up to do it. In

the future she'd ask for more details about the rooms
they had to share.

Matt was sitting in the chair at the small writing
table when Jenny came out of the bathroom. She
was wearing one of her T-shirts with the side slit to
accommodate the rope. He caught a glimpse of her
long legs as she approached.

"I'm done."

"I'll just be a minute. You know, we really ought
to do something to stay awake for another hour or
so, or our inner clocks are going to be very confused
at dawn."

"What did you have in mind?"

"How about a glass of wine on the balcony?"

Jenny looked at the sliding glass door that led to
a balcony with a decent view of the bay and some
of the old Victorian houses that were a landmark of
San Francisco. "That sounds lovely. I'll call
down—"

"I've already ordered from room service. You
can get the door if they come while I'm in the bathroom."

The wine and a selection of cheeses and fruit
came almost the moment Matt disappeared into the
bathroom, and Jenny had the bellboy set a table up
for them on the balcony. The bellboy ignored the
rope that led from Jenny's waist into the bathroom

with a nonchalance Jenny thought bellboys the world over must practice to perfection.

When Matt joined Jenny, he was wearing a pair of blue cotton pajama bottoms that were tied low on his hips. To her dismay, Jenny found Matt in pajamas every bit as sexy as Matt in next to nothing. His hair was still damp from his shower, and he smelled of soap and herbal shampoo.

"Shall we?" He gestured toward the balcony, and Jenny hurried ahead of him in an attempt to escape his alluring scent.

She didn't know when she'd ever enjoyed herself more. The light evening breeze was cool, but not cold, and she found the fog enchanting, probably because she didn't have to drive in it. The wine was crisp and dry, the cheese exotic, the fruit sweet, and the company...well, if Matt had set out to be charming, he'd certainly succeeded.

Jenny was starting to feel the lateness of the hour when Matt asked, "Will you tell me about your marriage, Jenny?"

She looked out toward the bay in an effort to avoid his discerning gaze. She let the city noises fill the quiet while she thought about how to answer him. At last she said, "It didn't end up being an altogether pleasant experience."

"What went wrong?"

Should she tell him? Maybe it would help him to understand her better. Jenny took a deep breath and said, "I got pregnant, Sam lost his job, and I got promoted, in that order."

"I didn't know you had a child," he said.

"I don't." Jenny hadn't meant to be curt, but she wasn't ready to talk about Sarah.

So, Matt thought. Jenny was like Adrienne. She hadn't wanted children, either. He was disappointed. He'd begun to think Jenny was different. This revelation proved she was as bad as the worst of the "liberated women." She'd obviously chosen her career ahead of having children.

Lost in her own memories, Jenny hadn't noticed Matt's silence. "How about you?" she asked. "What went wrong with your marriage?"

Matt gave a low laugh. "It's funny, but the whole time I was growing up, I always swore I wouldn't marry a woman like my mother. I wanted a woman who'd be willing to stay home and take care of a house and children and let me go out and earn a living. What I didn't realize was that all those years when I'd resented my mother for not being there, I'd also admired her for the work she did that took her away from us.

"When Adrienne came along, I was so captivated

by her intelligence, her ambition, her energy...I told myself it would work out.''

''But it didn't.''

Matt's voice was cynical when he replied, ''Hardly. When I suggested it was time we had children, Adrienne informed me in no uncertain terms that children weren't a part of her future.''

''Didn't you talk about having children before you got married?''

''Of course we did. Adrienne expressed some reservations, but, fool that I am, I thought she would change her mind—or that I would change it for her.''

''Typical man,'' Jenny intoned.

''I paid for it.''

''So why aren't you married to a housewife now, with three kids and another on the way?''

''I just haven't found the right woman. I'm not sure I ever will.''

''It's no wonder, if the women you date are all like Gerty,'' Jenny muttered.

Matt heard her and responded bitterly. ''You and people like you have pretty much done away with women who are ready to become the Happy Housewife. No self-respecting woman nowadays would be caught dead putting dinner on the table every evening for her husband and diapering her own babies.

They're all hung up on climbing the corporate ladder, working long hours so they can pay a housekeeper to take care of their husbands, house and home.''

Jenny responded to his pain by sharing her own. ''At one time I thought a man might appreciate a wife who had his children, even if she had to work, too. But I'm not convinced it's true anymore. I'm at the age now where I wish I had children.''

''If you're so gung ho on motherhood, why all this performance art with a feminist political theme? I don't understand, Jenny. It doesn't make sense.''

''I had a husband like you,'' Jenny explained. ''Before you flatter yourself that you're the kind of man I'd pick to marry, perhaps I should say that I found being married to a male chauvinist more than a little stifling. There's a fine line between a man who cares for a woman and one who's bent on taking care of her. I want a man who cares, but who'll accept me as an equal partner in a marriage.''

''Ahhh. So that's where you got the 'separate but equal' concept for this project.''

''I suppose so,'' Jenny conceded.

''What other attributes will this perfect marriage partner have?''

''I guess you saw all the romance novels on my bookshelf.''

Matt nodded.

"In every one there's a hero who's sensitive and thoughtful, but also strong—or maybe self-confident—enough to let the heroine be all she's destined to be. Is it so wrong to wish for a man like that in real life?"

"If you're looking for an ideal man, you're going to be disappointed. Real people have flaws. They're not perfect."

"Are you telling me I'm not going to find a sensitive, self-confident man out there somewhere?"

Matt smiled ruefully. "Guess you've got me there. If I say no, I denigrate the whole male sex. If I say yes...where does that leave us male chauvinist pigs?"

Jenny laughed. "You don't want to hear my answer to that. Honestly, Matt, I wouldn't have believed I could have such a rational discussion with someone as biased as you are against women."

"I must admit, you're the first liberated woman who's made any sense to me. Perhaps, on that convivial note, we should head for bed."

Jenny yawned. "Right. We've got a long afternoon tomorrow, and then a flight back to New York tomorrow evening."

After Jenny helped Matt turn down the bed, she gathered up the spread and rolled it into a tube long enough to run from the head to the foot of the mattress. "There. This side is mine. That side is yours. And the middle is no-man's land. Got it, Benson?"

"I got it, Smith. Loud and clear."

But once he was in bed, Matt couldn't sleep. Jenny was wide awake, too. There was an intimacy in the sleeping arrangements that wasn't conducive to rest.

Matt broke the wakeful silence with the startling question, "Who's paying for all this, Jenny?"

"Each of the galleries is picking up the costs of its respective performance," she answered. "In each case they've invited guests and special audiences, and then there'll be a certain time when the performance is open to the public."

"Do you really think these performances will make any difference in the greater scheme of things?"

Jenny could barely make out Matt's features in the moonlight that came through the sliding glass door. "If I didn't think so, I wouldn't do it."

There was a moment of silence before he said, "Good night, Jenny."

"Good night, Matt. I like your choice of pajamas."

Matt's grin appeared as a white flash in the darkness. The grin faded as he let himself wonder what it would have been like if he'd married a woman like Jenny instead of Adrienne. Jenny had said she wanted to fit a traditional female role and in the same breath said she wanted a partner who would be her equal. Were the two desires so irreconcilable? He knew from his past marriage that things were rarely ever equal between spouses. Could he give a woman the kind of freedom and support Jenny had said she needed to be happy? Matt sighed. Talk about moot issues. He was a chauvinist. She was a feminist. And never the twain shall meet.

Jenny heard Matt's sigh and knew exactly how he felt. There weren't any easy answers when it came to resolving such basic differences in attitudes as she and Matt had. But there was nothing that said she couldn't believe in miracles. And Jenny was pretty sure it was going to take a miracle to get rid of Matt's *oink*.

Six

I've never felt so humiliated in my entire life!''

They were on the plane home to New York from San Francisco, and Jenny was trying her best to calm Matt down without much success. "It's over and done with now. Why don't you forget it ever happened?''

"I'll never be able to face my colleagues again!''

"Come on, Matt. It couldn't be that bad.''

"Not that bad? Jerry Vanderwood, the critic from *Focus on Art*—our major competitor on the West Coast—was there laughing. Laughing!''

"Well, it *was* pretty funny.'' Jenny hid her grin

behind her hand. That was the last thing Matt needed to see, as riled up as he was.

"If I'd known what you'd planned, I never would have gone. How could you, Jenny?"

Jenny squelched the flicker of guilt she felt at Matt's accusation. A typical American living room had been recreated in a roped-off section of the gallery. At the moment in question, Jenny had been lying on the couch reading a book, and Matt had been sitting on the floor beside her, with his legs stretched out in front of him, watching television. "I knew the gallery was going to invite schoolchildren, but how could I know that little girl would be so outspoken? All she did—"

"All she did was make a fool of me!"

"Where's your sense of humor? All she said was that you looked cute, just like her puppy when he was on his leash. She didn't know that critic was standing right beside her." Jenny could still hear the childish voice piping up, "My puppy likes to watch television, too!"

A strangled sound issued from Matt's throat.

Fortunately, the flight attendant interrupted to ask, "Would either of you like something to drink?"

"I'd like some white wine," Jenny said.

"Jack Daniels," Matt choked. "And keep it coming."

Jenny let the Jack Daniels do what all her talking hadn't. By the time they reached New York, Matt appeared to have calmed down, but it was hard to tell, because he hadn't spoken for the rest of the trip.

Jenny knew the male ego was a fragile thing, but she'd never suspected Matt's could be crushed so easily. He was more vulnerable than she'd suspected, and she hoped that what had happened in San Francisco wasn't going to cause him to renege on his commitment to her project.

She gave directions to the cabbie who drove them back to her apartment. Matt followed her upstairs without a word and plopped down on the bed closest to the bathroom, throwing his forearm over his face with great melodrama.

By the time Jenny got out of the bathroom, Matt was sitting up in bed with the sheet draped across his waist.

"We have to talk," he said.

Jenny crossed to her bed and climbed in before she turned to Matt, her muscles tensed for the blow she felt sure was coming. "All right. Go ahead."

"I want to apologize. I guess I overreacted."

Jenny's whole body relaxed. "Does this mean you aren't backing out of the project?"

Matt leaned across the small table that separated him from Jenny. "I would be a fool if I gave up the chance to spend the next twenty-six nights sleeping next to you."

Jenny laughed with relief. "You're no kind of fool, Matt Benson. Anyone can see that."

"Can you, Jenny?"

"Of course." She laughed again, a nervous laugh this time, because he hadn't lain back down in his own bed yet.

"Then perhaps you'd agree to go to a football game with me on Thursday."

"What?"

"I have tickets for the Jets game on Thursday night. Would you like to go?"

Jenny laughed, a joyous sound. "You didn't have to ask me. You know I'd have to go anyway."

"But I want you to be my date."

Jenny was stunned. Matt thought maybe he'd gone too far and was on the verge of withdrawing his request when she drawled, "Why, Matthew Benson, I do believe you're hustling a feminist."

This time it was Matt's turn to laugh. "Why, *Ms.* Smith, I do believe you're right."

That encounter set the tone for the rest of the week, which passed more pleasantly than either of them could have hoped.

The reviews from the San Francisco newspapers were, if not glowing, at least very positive. Jenny would have to wait another week for the review from *Focus on Art*, but if the papers were any guide, she didn't have anything to worry about. She read to Matt:

...part of the critic's job is to discern whether performance art speaks to the audience for which it is intended. In *Separate but Equal*, artist Jennifer Smith asks us to believe a premise that many would not espouse wholeheartedly today. By her choice of subject matter alone, she forces us to confront our consciences on the matter of sexual equality. If she does no more than that, she has done enough.

"Don't get your hopes up that Jerry Vanderwood will be so supportive," Matt warned. "He's a dyed-in-the-wool male chauvinist."

"And you're not?"

"No, I donned my hair shirt later in life."

Jenny was silent for a moment while she considered the import of what Matt had just admitted. If what he said was true, perhaps it was possible for him to shed his prejudice as easily as doffing a wool coat when springtime came around again. "At any rate," Jenny said, "I'm not going to mope around all week worrying about it. It's enough of a coup for me to have simply gotten him to come in the first place.''

In Tuesday's class, Matt joined the discussion regarding which should be saved from a fire, an old man or Da Vinci's *Mona Lisa*, offering Jenny's students food for thought when he suggested they alter the problem slightly. What if the man was very ill and was going to die anyway? Which would they save then? Or what if they had to choose between saving the *Mona Lisa* or saving a cat? As a living being, did the cat deserve more consideration than a priceless work of art? Or did the fact it was ''only a cat'' make its life of negligible value?

The discussion had been lively, and Matt had helped them work toward the answer Jenny had reached long ago. An artist shouldn't sacrifice everything—marriage, family, happiness, even hearth and home—for art. Being an artist was important, but having a good life was even more so.

Matt was pleasantly surprised on Thursday to discover that Jenny was a Jets fan. ''You never told me you love football,'' Matt shouted to her over the crowd noise in the stadium in New Jersey's Meadowlands complex.

''You never asked!'' she shouted back with a grin. Then she was jumping up and yelling again, because the wide receiver had caught a long bomb.

"Did you see that?" she screamed. "Wow! First and goal at the three-yard line. Come on, Jets!"

Jenny was no less enthusiastic when the Jets had to settle for a field goal, shouting as the ball changed hands, "*De*-fense! *De*-fense!"

Matt was once again stymied by the incongruities in Jenny's behavior. Feminists weren't supposed to enjoy football. Were they?

Later that evening, in bed, Jenny was still bubbly with excitement. "What a game! I couldn't believe that pass in the third quarter. And the run that followed it, well, we'll be seeing that one again for the next twenty years or so when they do the recaps on TV."

"How did you learn to like football, Jenny?"

"My father loved the game. I guess I started watching at his knee and came to love it as much as he did." Jenny grinned at him. "Lots of women love football, Matt. We can be just as bloodthirsty and competitive as any man."

"But you don't look like—"

"People rarely fit into the pigeonholes you try to put them in. That's one of the reasons I wanted you to spend time with me on this project, so you could see how true that is of both men and women."

"Is Jason one of those people who doesn't fit into a pigeonhole?" Matt asked.

Although the question had come out of left field, Jenny sensed the underlying curiosity and concern about her relationship with her partner. "Jason's life hasn't been predictable, if that's what you're asking. He used to be a football player, a good one. He got injured and had to leave the game. He's one of those people who never learned the lesson I'm trying to teach my students. He'd sacrificed everything for football, and when he couldn't play anymore, he had nothing left to live for. It took him a long time to come to grips with his life. It was especially hard because what he discovered he wanted to do wasn't something anyone expects of an ex-football player. He took a lot of ribbing from some of his former teammates. But many of them stood by him, and now he's a successful, happy human being."

"I see. And how much did you personally have to do with Jason's self-discovery?"

"Not much, really. When he was looking for a studio I had a whole loft to myself and—"

"—and you offered to share it with him. That was very generous, Jenny. Not at all competitive and bloodthirsty."

She flushed. "I've never been sorry."

"I never suggested you were."

The tension between them, which had been absent all week, suddenly returned. Jenny was conscious again of the fact that she was sharing her bedroom with a man she'd known only seven days. After all they'd been through together, she could hardly call Matthew Benson a stranger. Yet there were so many things they didn't know about one another, so many spots of quicksand that could catch one or the other unaware and leave them sinking into the mire.

Jenny shivered and pulled the sheet up over her shoulders.

"Are you cold?"

"No, I just... I'm tired. It's been a long day. Good night, Matt."

"Good night, Jenny."

Matt's husky voice sent another shiver down Jenny's spine. He'd acted the role of good friend all week. Maybe he'd been trying the relationship on for size, Jenny thought, and it hadn't fit. Because the look in Matt's eyes just now had been much more than friendly concern.

Matt stared at the cold shoulder Jenny had turned to him. What had happened to change everything so quickly? He hadn't consciously said or done anything provocative, had he? But he had let her see that he admired her, had even spoken of his admiration. Surely friends could admire one another. And Jenny was his friend, at least as much as someone could be on seven days' acquaintance. He was trying hard not to want more from her, but it wasn't easy.

The truth of the matter was, he wanted to be Jenny Smith's lover.

Their fragile friendship was sorely tested by the trip to the Chicago gallery over the weekend, which was a nightmare of mishaps. The plane was delayed out of Kennedy, then delayed again before it could land at O'Hare. The hotel room had double beds, all right, but Jenny had eaten something on the plane that disagreed with her stomach, so Matt spent most of the night sitting outside the bathroom door, which was on the opposite side of the room from the beds.

There was a cold snap in Chicago, and neither Jenny nor Matt had brought cold-weather clothes. The gallery wasn't heated, so they spent an uncomfortable afternoon being ogled by patrons bundled up in hats and sweaters. Jenny suffered in silence through the performance, then let Matt drag her back to the airport, where they waited in vain for a flight that was finally canceled. They ended up taking a cab to a hotel located near the airport.

In the hotel's sundry shop Jenny found a copy of the most recent *Focus on Art*. She forced herself to wait until they were in their room to open the magazine and read the review of *Separate but Equal*. Jerry Vanderwood's critique was scathing.

Matt could see from Jenny's grim features that the review wasn't good. He took the magazine from her and read, "'To a world full of tripe, performance artist Jennifer Smith has added yet another piece of feminist rubbish.'" It was strictly downhill from there.

"I'm sorry, Jenny," Matt said when he'd finished reading it. He closed the distance between them until he was standing next to her in the middle of the room. "It's just one opinion."

"But an important one," she replied bitterly. "You said yourself, he's your major competition. That means he has a large readership. Oh, Matt! Can he possibly be right?"

"This doesn't sound like the Jenny I've known for the past thirteen days. Where's your fighting spirit?" He yearned to reach out and comfort her, to lift her chin and infuse her with some of his own strength. He wondered if she'd felt this bad when she'd read his review of *Woman at a Party*. He sure hoped not. She looked absolutely miserable. "You can't let a little thing like this get you down."

"I'm tired, Matt. Please, would you turn down the sheets for me? I think if I don't lie down, I'm going to topple over."

Her cheeks looked feverishly pink. "Are you sure you don't have a temperature?" Matt started to lay his hand on Jenny's brow. At the last second he realized what he was doing and stopped himself. Jenny was too far gone to even notice.

In fact, she was so far gone that she undressed right there beside the bed, seemingly unaware that she was exposing the flat plane of her stomach above her silk bikini panties and the rosy nipples barely hidden by the lace of her bra.

Matt slapped down his unruly libido and tucked Jenny into bed, resisting the temptation to climb in after her.

"Did I ever tell you," Jenny murmured, "what I thought when I first saw you?"

Matt wondered if she were in shock. But when she opened her hazel eyes, they were clear. Whatever she was about to say wasn't being said unawares. "No. You never did. Are you going to tell me now?"

"Yes." Jenny's eyes closed, her lush lashes lying against her cheeks. She was practically asleep, Matt realized, and maybe not as aware of what she was saying as he'd believed.

"I thought you were the most handsome man I'd ever...you reminded me of the heroes in my books, with your broad shoulders and your lean hips, your

steely gray eyes and your shaggy black hair.''
Jenny's eyes remained closed, but her smile broadened. ''I had to admit you weren't a creep after all.''

''A creep?'' Matt sputtered.

Jenny's eyes opened, full of mischief. ''After I read your review of *Woman at a Party* I called you a lot of names. Creep was one of the nicer ones.''

''But I reminded you of a hero when you met me?''

''Physically, yes. Tonight…tonight you remind me of the other thing I like about those romantic heroes. Once in a while it's nice to let someone else handle things. I suppose that's one of the good things about being part of a pair. When one half is down the other half can…take up…the slack.''

As she spoke, Jenny slowly but surely collected the rope that lay between them until Matt was leaning over her with his face inches from hers.

Just what do you think you're doing, Jennifer Smith!

I want him to kiss me. I want him to hold me in his arms.

What about your project, Jenny?

To hell with it! I can't stand the tension anymore.

You'll regret this tomorrow.

No, I won't. How could I regret fulfilling my heart's desire?

Aren't you exaggerating just a little?

Jenny ignored the little voice that warned her she was making a mistake. Her eyes focused on Matt's mouth, which had parted, and she watched avidly as his tongue slowly dampened his lower lip. Then her eyes met his, and she found all the wanting there that she was experiencing herself. Heat pooled in her belly, and the tips of her breasts budded with need.

Matt recognized Jenny's sensual response to his gaze. His own body was responding with equal alacrity.

"Jenny, we can't do this."

"Why not?"

"You'll be sorry in the morning."

"No, I won't. Please, Matt."

Matt's teeth itched to clamp down on Jenny's pouting lower lip. "No, I—"

Matt lowered his head until he could feel Jenny's breath on his face. Then something stopped him.

Touching Jenny now would mean the end of any chance for a retraction of his negative review.

A small voice inside him argued, but she asked you to touch her. She begged, just the way you knew she would. So, kiss her! Kiss her, now!

Abruptly, Matt jerked away. "Oh, God, I must be a crazy man, but I can't take advantage of you like this. You're exhausted. You're hurting. You don't know what you're doing.''

Matt told himself all the reasons why he shouldn't do what he wanted to do, but nothing calmed the throbbing need he felt. He fumbled a cigarette out of the pack and lit it with his silver lighter. He inhaled and waited for the nicotine to hit his system.

Jenny turned away and curled into a fetal ball. She felt the hot tears on her cheeks and thought maybe Matt was right and she was merely suffering the effects of exhaustion. Surely she couldn't be crying because Matt Benson, chauvinist, destroyer of artistic careers, heartless creep—who'd most recently been acting suspiciously like the hero of her dreams—hadn't wanted to make love to her.

They were both wan with fatigue when they boarded the plane the next morning for New York.

Jenny had spent the night regretting her lamentable lapse in control.

Matt had spent the night regretting his disgusting sense of nobility.

''I have an exhibit to review this afternoon,'' he announced as the plane was landing at Kennedy.

Jenny groaned. She hadn't slept at all the previous night, and she was pretty sure Matt hadn't either.

Yet there was no way to get a respite from one another's company. How long could they last like this?

By the time they got back to her apartment after attending the exhibit, they didn't speak, just headed for the bedroom, which had become a haven for them both.

"It's good to be home," Matt said.

Jenny smiled. "Yes. It is. We'd better get to bed. I've got class early tomorrow."

This time it was Matt who wanted to groan. "Fourteen days down after tomorrow, sixteen to go. I'll be glad when this damned project is over."

That comment set the tone for the coming week. Neither of them slept well, so their fatigue built to monumental proportions. Their appetites suffered. And everything was an irritant, abrading the fragile shell of polite behavior that was all that kept them from murdering each other.

"You left toothpaste in the sink again."

"If it bothers you so much, wipe it up."

"I'm smoking a cigarette tonight, and if you don't like it, you can lump it."

"When I die of cancer from inhaling your lousy smoke, it'll be on your head."

* * *

"Will you please pick up your blasted under-shorts!"

"Step over them."

"Is this the best coffee you can make?"

"If it tastes like poison, it's probably because I wish it was!"

Jenny knew she was being a shrew, but there didn't seem to be anything she could do about it. Neither one of them had been acting much like an adult for the past few days. She could find no other explanation for her behavior than the fact that she was going crazy from spending the past sixteen days no farther than ten feet away from Matt. Human beings weren't meant to live in each other's pockets like this without touching. It appeared that Matt was also being driven insane by their enforced proximity.

Matt was down to his last shred of tolerance. He thought perhaps what they both needed was a change of scene. "We're going to have dinner at my house tonight."

"I didn't know you had a house," Jenny snapped.

"Well, I do! We can take the train from Penn station and be on Long Island in half an hour." Thinking Jenny might be reluctant to go and desperate to get her agreement, he added, "I have to go there anyway to pick up the artist's supplies I need for the United Way benefit next Saturday. So we might as well go now.''

''What artist's supplies? What United Way benefit?''

''I thought I told you about it.''

''No, you didn't.''

Matt bit back a terrible word he had no business saying in front of a lady and instead carefully explained, ''There's a United Way benefit for supporters of the arts. I've agreed to sell caricatures of the personalities who attend, with all the money going to the United Way.''

''I didn't know you did caricatures.''

''There's a lot you don't know about me,'' he replied cynically. ''We'll spend tonight at my place and catch the train back into the city tomorrow in plenty of time to make our flight to Houston. Want to go?''

Jenny was feeling just petulant enough to say no, but what came out was, ''Sure.''

They caught the train that afternoon, picking up Matt's car where he'd left it parked near the station and driving the rest of the way to his house, which was located on a tree-shaded lane in Roslyn Heights. It was a split-level, with a big bay window in front. Tasteful, comfortable, just the sort of suburban home where one might find a wife, 2.3 children and a dog. In Matt's case, he only had the dog.

"That's Spot," Matt said as he explained the appearance of an excited dalmatian barking at the fence. "My neighbor's been taking care of him for me while I've been staying in the city with you."

Matt opened the door and gestured Jenny inside ahead of him. She stopped at the entry to the living room and stared at her surroundings in awe. The furniture consisted of large, masculine pieces in earth tones, from buff to brown, from rust to burnt sienna. The room had a slightly cluttered, lived-in look. There were old gallery programs everywhere. A beer can sat next to a full ashtray on the coffee table, and a baseball cap perched on the lamp shade. "It's so…warm."

The house had been closed up, and Matt moved quickly to adjust the climate control. "It'll cool off soon."

Jenny turned and caught the end of what he was saying. "No, you didn't understand. I meant, your home, it's so cozy. It gives me a warm feeling inside."

Matt smiled at Jenny, a smile that offered all the warmth of the man and melted the coldness that had existed between them all week. "Come on. Let me show you the rest of the place."

"How many bedrooms do you have?"

"Three upstairs, one downstairs. I use the downstairs bedroom for guests. Although, in this case, I guess you'll have to stay upstairs with me," Matt said with the first grin that had touched his face in a week.

Jenny headed straight for the colorful fall New England landscape above the fireplace. It was signed "Benson." "This is a wonderful painting, Matt." She turned to face him. "Why did you quit?"

He shrugged. "I knew I'd never be great. Being good wasn't good enough for me." Uncomfortable with Jenny's questioning, he offered again, "Want to see the rest of the house?"

"I'd love to."

Jenny strongly felt the loss of Sarah when she entered an upstairs bedroom that was obviously intended for children. "I can see how it would have been a disappointment when your wife didn't want to have children. This room—"

"My nieces and nephews stay here when they come to visit," Matt interrupted.

Jenny followed Matt to his bedroom. The first thing she noticed was the king-size bed. On the opposite side of the room, a desk sat facing a large picture window that opened on a backyard barbecue and a pool.

"I planned to watch my kids playing in the back-yard from here," Matt murmured, running his hand along the smooth cherry wood of the desk.

"Why did you keep the house?" Jenny asked. "After you divorced, I mean. Isn't it a little large for a single man?"

Matt looked sheepish. "I guess I never gave up hoping that someday I'd fill it with my kids." He ran his hand through his hair nervously. "That's enough of that. I'm hungry."

"Is the kitchen stocked?"

"We ought to be able to throw something to-gether out of what's in the freezer."

They ate filet mignon by candlelight in the dining room, washing the food down with a cabernet sauvi-gnon.

"I wish it were cooler," Matt said. "I'd light a fire, and we could retire to the living room with a brandy."

"We can still have the brandy, can't we?" Jenny asked, catching his glance over the rim of her wine glass.

He swallowed hard. The tension they'd fought all week had changed. He wasn't sure what was hap-pening between them; he only knew he was damned confused. "Sure. Just let me clean up—"

"We can do that together later, can't we?" She

rose and sauntered into the living room, giving Matt a ''come hither'' look as she passed him.

If he hadn't known better, he would have thought Jenny was making a pass at him. But, of course, it had to be his imagination.

Jenny settled herself on the couch and waited for Matt to pour their brandies. Everything she'd ever wanted from a home was in this house, including the husband who wanted children. So what was she going to do about it?

Seven

Matt didn't know exactly what was going on in Jenny's head, but he wasn't about to argue with the intimate scene she'd arranged for them in the living room—the two of them sitting on the couch, soft candlelight, and a good glass of brandy. Jenny was a beautiful woman, and he was more than willing to satisfy any urges she wanted satisfied tonight.

The problem was, her contradictory signals left him totally confused. He took advantage of one of her "yes" signals to move closer to her on the couch. The instant he did, she backed away from him.

Definitely a "no."

Before he had a chance to get discouraged, she slipped off the couch to a spot on the floor beside him, then turned to face him, with her hands laced together on the couch not an inch from his thigh.

That was a "yes."

But as he edged his thigh closer to her hand she shifted again, this time to sprawl back against a hassock, with her legs spread wide on either side of his feet.

Was that a "yes" or a "no"?

Matt was a patient man, and he'd been teased by the best of them. But he'd been aroused even before he'd come into the room with Jenny, and the sight of her sprawled spread-legged across from him had left him hard and ready. He wanted her to make up her mind one way or the other.

There were several more "yes" overtures, all of which Matt answered, so that when the "I've changed my mind about the whole thing" signal came, it tipped him over the edge.

"That's it!"

"What's wrong?"

"Don't act so innocent, Jenny. You know damn well what's wrong!"

"I don't!" she protested.

Matt stuck a finger under Jenny's nose and raged,

"If I touch you without your say-so I have to print a retraction. But you've been doing your damnedest to make sure I touch you!"

"I haven't!"

"If you choose to keep yourself tied up in sexual knots, that's your business, but don't make me a part of your games."

"I wasn't playing!"

Matt was on a roll, and he wasn't about to let Jenny's helpless innocent act get in the way of his rampage. "If you want to deny yourself the pleasure of sex for the rest of your life, fine!"

"I never—"

"After this little show, all I can say is that your husband must have been glad to be rid of you!"

"It wasn't me Sam wanted to be rid of! It was our baby!" Jenny shrieked.

Matt was stunned by Jenny's outburst. He exhaled a deep sigh, filling the terrible silence. "Jenny, I didn't know. I thought—"

Jenny wasn't even listening to Matt. She was caught up in the nightmare of the past. "He said to get rid of her, but I didn't! I kept her, and I loved her until she...until she died." Jenny's breath caught on a sob, and she turned away from Matt, hiding her face in her hands.

In light of her revelation, he felt guilty as hell for

yelling at her. But his anger still smoldered, because, despite this abrupt change in the direction of the evening's conversation, something had been happening between him and Jenny tonight. Could she really not have known what she'd been doing to him?

But with the heat of the moment past, Jenny's protests of innocence struck a chord of reality. And he suspected that only extreme agitation—the result of innocence in the face of his accusations, perhaps—could have driven her to reveal the truth about her child.

Matt had to admit that he hadn't been angry with Jenny simply because she'd been teasing him and then had said no. A lot of women had said no in the past, and he hadn't flown off the handle like this. No, the reason he'd been so angry was because he didn't know whether she'd really wanted him, or whether she'd just been using him to get her damned retraction. While his feelings—and he wasn't willing to define them too carefully—were genuine, he feared hers weren't.

Right now he wanted to reach out and comfort her, but after all the things he'd just said, that was the last thing he could do. He crouched down behind her, careful not to brush against her, and offered the only solace he could. "If you want to talk about it, Jenny, I'm here to listen."

Jenny tucked her legs underneath her as she turned warily toward Matt. "Why should I trust you after the way you just yelled at me?"

"Please, Jenny."

She reached for her glass of brandy and took a swallow as she considered his plea for forgiveness. "All right," she said at last.

He sagged down beside her, so they were both leaning back against the couch. But it took a while longer before Jenny was able to talk. Matt watched as she ran her fingers agitatedly through her hair, smoothed her rumpled blouse and rubbed her sweaty hands together. Finally she spoke.

"Sarah was the reason I divorced my husband," she began. "Sam wasn't ready for children, so I raised Sarah by myself. She was four years old when she died. That was five years ago." Jenny took another sip of brandy. "She had a rare kind of childhood leukemia, and the symptoms didn't show up right away. When they did, the doctors didn't give me much hope. They told me she might have six months. She only had four."

Matt watched helplessly as the tears pooled in Jenny's eyes. Now he understood very well her obsession with time. Despite the tragedy she'd unfolded for him, he was filled with hope. Because the fact that Jenny had lost her child meant that at some point she'd made the choice to become a mother. He wanted to hold her in his arms and soothe away her pain, but he couldn't even reach out a warm hand in comfort. Words didn't seem like enough, but they were all he was allowed.

"I'm..." He cleared his throat and tried again. "I'm so sorry, Jenny."

He didn't know whether she heard him or not. She seemed to be caught in a web of pain. He kept his promise and listened as she admitted, "I don't think about her all the time anymore. But every once in a while something will trigger a memory, and she's there, laughing, smiling, telling me how much she loves me...being brave for Mommy."

Matt couldn't help himself. He reached out to her.

"Don't! Don't touch me!" she rasped, shrinking away from his outstretched fingertips.

"Jenny, let me share the hurt. Let me—"

"*No!* You said you wouldn't touch me unless I asked you to, Matt. My project—"

"Damn your project! Are you forgetting your own lessons?" he snapped. "Or was that all just so much rhetoric? I thought you believed what you taught. *Art is important, but life is more important.* Let me help, Jenny."

Her brow furrowed in confusion.

When it was apparent that she wasn't going to reach out to him, he said, "At least tell me what I can do to help you, Jenny, if I can't touch you."

His soft, husky plea reached her at last, and she turned and focused on his darkened gray eyes, his rigidly out-thrust chin. She felt a wave of comfort flowing over her. "I think you already have helped, simply by listening. I've never told anyone else what I just told you. I guess I needed to get all that out, but somehow there was never anybody..."

"I'm glad you chose me."

"Me too," Jenny said with a watery smile. "Sarah's buried in a cemetery outside Houston. I'd like to go visit her when we're there over the weekend."

"Sure." Matt reached out to take her brandy snifter, careful not to brush her hand. "Come on. It's time to go to bed. We've got to get up early tomorrow to catch the train back into the city."

He led her upstairs and waited patiently outside the bathroom door until she'd changed into her T-shirt. Then he stepped into the bathroom himself. When he came out he was wearing a pair of maroon silk pajama bottoms.

"Pajamas?"

"It's going to be hard enough to sleep in this bed

tonight without touching you, Jenny. I need all the help I can get.''

Jenny should have been offended by Matt's announcement. Instead she felt unaccountably pleased. She hadn't forgotten that his outrage had resulted from her ambivalence toward having him touch her, so she quickly slipped under the covers, careful not to tease him unnecessarily. She turned on her side, facing away from him, and he did the same with her. The vast expanse of the king-size bed yawned like an abyss between them.

Jenny closed her eyes and inhaled the scent of Matt's masculine cologne that lingered on the pillowcase. The time would soon come when she would have to confront the question of whether her attraction to Matt was anything more than the natural result of forcing two healthy adults to sleep in the same bedroom night after night without allowing events to follow to their natural conclusion.

Matt lay wide awake, wondering. What did Jenny want from him? Perhaps more to the point, what did he want from her? Somehow his feelings for her had passed far beyond mere sexual wanting, even though that was all he'd been able to express to her. But how could he possibly spend the rest of his life tied to a woman like Jenny? He might have donned his

chauvinist cloak late in life, but he wasn't so sure it
would be that easy to shrug it off.

Still, what Jenny offered was tantalizing enough
to make Matt begin to hope and dream again. He
heard the joyful sounds of children's laughter. He
saw the faces of his sons and daughters, radiant with
happiness. He smelled the musky scent of his wife
after making love to her on the bed in this room.
And he ached for the dream to become reality.

Jenny was on a plane with Matt, bound for Houston.
She fought the desire to glance at her watch. She'd
expected the morning after she'd teased Matt un-
mercifully, then bared her soul, to be awkward and
uncomfortable, but he had made sure it wasn't.
They'd taken a giant step toward becoming friends,
and she was determined to enjoy the nine days she
had left in his company without counting the
minutes and hours. From bitter experience she knew
that that would only lead to frustration and unhap-
piness.

"Houston strikes me as a city that should greet a
feminist project with hospitality," Matt said.

"Why do you say that?"

"Isn't it the city where Billie Jean King whipped
Bobby Riggs at tennis?"

Jenny laughed. "Sure, and if you think even one

Texas cowboy believed before the match began that Bobby wouldn't swat Billie Jean back into the kitchen where she belonged, you're not as well-informed a chauvinist as I thought."

"I suppose you're right," Matt agreed with a chuckle. "After all, Texas is the land of the good ole country music boys, isn't it?"

"Not to mention roughnecks, truckers and football," Jenny added with a wry grin.

"How did you get to Texas? And from there to New York?"

"Sam got a job offer in Houston, and we decided to live in the suburbs. I stayed there when Sam and I split up. But when Sarah died, I wanted to get away from all the memories, so I decided to pursue my artistic career in the Big Apple. I was naive enough to believe I was going to wake up the world with my art."

"You haven't done such a bad job at that."

Jenny sensed they were on dangerous ground and changed the focus to Matt. "What about you? How did you end up in New York?"

"Small-town boy from Iowa seeks fame and fortune—"

"No! You can't be from Iowa. You're too... too..."

"Too suave and debonair? Too good in bed?"

Jenny laughed. "The former, maybe. The latter..."

"You'll have to give me a chance to prove myself one way or the other," Matt said with a predatory gleam in his eyes.

Jenny met his gaze and acknowledged that the time would come when he'd get his wish. But not until the full month of September had passed. Right now the success of her project—and acquiring Matt's retraction—were the most important considerations.

More important than a future with Matt?

Matt hasn't offered anything.

He's offered himself.

The subject isn't even up for discussion until the project's finished.

So, which is more important, Jenny, life or art?

Art. All right, life! Stop trying to confuse me.

Matt felt an immediate physical response to the flare of desire in Jenny's hazel eyes. He shifted to get more comfortable.

"Something wrong?" Jenny questioned coyly.

"Now, Jenny, don't tease," Matt said. "I'm trying very hard to be good."

"I'm sure you are."

Matt stared blankly at her for a moment and then groaned at her innuendo.

Jenny giggled, a totally feminine sound. She had actually been teasing him about sex, this liberated woman. Matt felt an unaccountable yearning for…something. He could imagine waking up to her face in the morning. At the same time, he didn't know how he'd be able to stand living with her.

She would expect him to stop leaving toothpaste in the sink and to throw his undershorts in the laundry instead of on the floor. She would expect him to quit smoking. She would expect him to let her keep working. She would expect him to do his share in the kitchen. She would want him to leave the light on at night so she could read. Was he willing at this late date to make all those changes in his life just so he could be with Jenny?

"Penny for your thoughts?"

Matt smiled blandly and replied, "I hope it's not too muggy in Houston."

"Oh." Why had she thought he might be contemplating more weighty things—like their relationship with each other? Matt had let her know that he wanted her, but he'd never said he wanted to spend his life with her. And why should he? She didn't know two people who were more unsuited to living with one another. Hadn't the past two and a half weeks together more than proved that?

You could change.

Me? Or Matt?

Both. There's always compromise, you know.

Why should I have to change? I've been perfectly happy as I am. He smokes; I don't. He's a slob; I'm neat. He's a morning person; I stay up late at nights. He expects me to wait on him; I want him to share the load.

I'm not going to argue with you, Jenny. The decision is up to you.

You bet it is!

It was two very solemn individuals who debarked at Houston's Hobby International Airport. But their sober moods didn't last beyond the lengthy drive in a rental car from the airport to the hotel.

"There's no such thing as a short drive in Houston," Jenny joked to Matt. "Somebody once told me an entire northeastern state could fit inside the Houston city limits." When they finally reached the hotel, Jenny was wide awake and raring to go. "Why don't we go to Gilley's?"

"At this hour of the night?"

"Who's watching the time?" Jenny quipped. "Come on, Matt, please? Believe it or not, in all the time I lived here, I never went there, even though it's a country-and-western landmark—you know, the same way most New Yorkers have never visited the Empire State Building or the Statue of Liberty. It was just too much trouble to fight the crowds to go dancing and listen to the music."

Matt held up the rope between them in exasperation. "And you pick *now* to fight crowds?"

Jenny laughed. "It'll be fun. I know I'll never be able to get any sleep. I'm too keyed up. What do you say?"

"I say you're crazy, lady. But, all right, let's go!"

At the height of its popularity, Gilley's had been a mecca for tourists as well as a watering hole for "regulars." It boasted a huge dance floor and a mechanical bull that tested the patrons' balance and sobriety.

Jenny's mood was infectious, and before he'd had his second beer, Matt was laughing and tapping his foot to the fiddler's rendition of a Texas folk dance, the Cotton-eyed Joe. By the time Matt was well into his third beer, Jenny even had him singing along to a country tune.

"Lookee here, Clete. This gent done lassoed himself a pretty little heifer. Got her tied up good and tight."

Matt turned an amused eye toward the redneck cowboys who'd come up behind him and Jenny. The one who'd spoken had a huge lump of chewing tobacco in his cheek. Matt saw the outline of the tobacco tin in the hip pocket of the man's well-worn jeans and knew the paper cup in his hand wasn't full of soda. The cowboy set his scuffed boot on the back rung of Matt's bar stool and demanded, "What fer ya got the li'l lady all tied up like that, mister?"

"None of your business," Matt replied amiably. He tipped up his beer and swallowed the cool brew.

The man called Clete sidled up closer to Matt in an attempt to separate him from Jenny. "My friend, Slim, done asked ya a question, mister."

"And I gave him an answer."

Jenny could see that Matt was enjoying himself. Didn't he know these rednecks were itching for a fight? While he might enjoy the brawl, he wasn't exactly free to indulge himself. "I'm ready to go, Matt."

Abruptly Slim stepped up to block Jenny's exit. "Where ya goin', honey? I ain't had a chance to dance with ya yet."

Jenny raised herself to her full five feet nine inches and gestured to the rope that tied her to Matt. "As you can see, my man is on the possessive side. If you were to raise a finger to me, if you were to so much as breathe hard on me," she drawled, "why, I'm afraid he'd be inclined to make you very sorry."

Slim glanced quickly at Matt, as though to judge whether there was any truth behind the pretty blond-haired woman's words. Matt stood, and at a broad-shouldered six feet three inches, there was a lot of him to provide intimidation. "My woman spoke her piece. You got any more questions?"

"No, sir, I ain't," Slim said quickly. "Come on, Clete. Let's go get a beer."

As soon as the cowboys left, Jenny turned to Matt, her hazel eyes flashing with anger. "Just what did you think you were doing, provoking them like that? Clete had a knife hanging on his belt, and cowboys like him are always looking to draw blood."

"So you unsheathed your claws first, hmm?" Matt said with a mellow smile.

Jenny was furious at his total lack of concern. "Have you heard a word I've said?"

Matt leaned closer, nose to nose with Jenny. "I heard every single word you said. As a man who's *on the possessive side*, I'd say I behaved remarkably well. Never even lifted a finger to either one of those fellows," he said with a rakish grin.

"Oooo. You…you…macho man!"

He laughed, his voice husky, low and sexy, and Jenny felt a frisson of desire skitter up her spine.

Matt had told her once that she was beautiful when she was angry. He hadn't changed his mind. He found her more desirable than words could describe. He leaned over and whispered in her ear,

"Let's go back to the hotel, Jenny. Let me hold you in my arms. I want to taste you with my lips and tongue. I want to suckle your breasts. I want to put my hands on you and inside you and make you moan with pleasure. I want to join us together, to slide deep inside you, to have you hold me there and make us one. Let me love you, Jenny. Come back—"

"Matt, please stop." It was a cry of both denial and desire. "I can't! Don't torture us both like this!"

In a blind panic, Jenny ran.

Matt cursed the two beers that had loosened his tongue, cursed the need that drove him to speak, cursed the self-control that allowed Jenny to deny them both.

The rope stopped her, of course, but not before there was a significant crowd separating them. She struggled toward the exit, and Matt followed her as best he could, shoving people aside, countering the confusion as people realized there was a rope entangling them with the man who was trying to get by.

Once outside Jenny sucked in a breath of the cool, refreshing night air, then another one, before turning to confront Matt, who was only moments behind her. They walked side by side toward the rental car they'd parked in the large lot. Matt slipped inside and scooted over behind the wheel, then waited for Jenny to get settled before he said, "Jenny, I apologize."

"Why should you be sorry? You weren't saying anything I haven't thought myself."

Matt hissed out the breath of air he'd been holding. "You never said anything before."

"Why should I make it harder on both of us?" Jenny sought out Matt's eyes in the moonlight. "I want you every bit as much as you want me, Matt. I have since the first day I saw you. Maybe when my project is over and done with..." Left unsaid was *When you've printed a retraction.* "If you still feel the same way..."

"I'll always want you, Jenny."

Jenny wondered if he was being honest with himself. Always was a long time.

When they got back to their room Matt thanked heaven for twin beds, turned his back on Jenny in her T-shirt that drove him crazy and muttered to himself, "Just ignore her legs and you'll be fine."

Jenny smiled, but bit back the smart-alecky retort on her tongue. She wondered whether there was any more to Matt's feelings for her than desire. Or was the stipulation for a retraction they'd agreed upon fueling his libido?

The differences in life-style that stood between

them had precluded her probing her own feelings further. What if she discovered that she loved him, but couldn't stand to live with him? She knew that happened more often than people were willing to admit. Maybe a smart-alecky remark wasn't such a bad idea after all. At least it might help relieve the tension. She turned to Matt and whispered, "I think your legs are kind of nice, too."

Matt groaned. "Jenny, have some mercy. My willpower is only so strong."

"Good night, Matt. You're beautiful when you're angry."

"Trite, Jenny."

"True, Matt."

The reviews in the Houston papers on Monday morning were all positive. In fact, two of them were glowing. Matt attributed that to the fact all three critics were women. In consideration of Jenny's obvious distraction after their visit to the cemetery to place flowers on Sarah's grave, Matt didn't pursue the matter during the flight home.

However, once they were settled in bed in Jenny's apartment that evening, he brought the subject up for discussion.

"Are you suggesting those three women critics are all *gender biased*?" Jenny questioned. "And that if I'd been a man making the same presentation, the reviews would have been different?''

"If you'd been a man, you never would have made this particular presentation.''

"You're not back to that 'artists paint what they know' theory, are you?'' Jenny demanded.

"I'm afraid so.''

"Matt, you've spent nearly three weeks with me. Are you still on square one? Haven't you moved an inch in any direction?''

"I'll say this, Jenny. If I'm suggesting that those three women are gender biased, perhaps I'm also willing to agree that I'm gender biased, as well.''

Jenny blinked twice. "You are? I mean, of course you are. Gender biased, that is. I knew it when I read your review of *Woman at a Party*. Now we're making some progress. Are you willing to print a retraction now?''

"No, I'm not.''

Jenny scooted over to the edge of her bed on her knees. "Why not?''

"I'm not convinced I was wrong.''

"Of course you were wrong! You just admitted you were already biased against me because I was a woman before you ever came to see my performance. What kind of fair evaluation could you make under those circumstances?''

The hair was standing up on the back of Matt's neck. He didn't know exactly how Jenny had managed to rile him, but his good humor had vanished. "We don't live in a vacuum. A person—male or female—is never going to be completely neutral."

"Then I'd settle for having you admit that your review reflected a sexual bias."

"I'll just bet you would!"

"You unreasonable, stubborn—"

"Can it, Jenny!"

Jenny leapt off the bed and paced back and forth at the length of her tether, her temper simmering.

Every time she turned, the tail of her T-shirt flipped up, giving Matt an enticing glimpse of her slender legs and silken underwear. She must know how arousing her behavior was, so why did she do it?

"What are you really angry about, Jenny? Does this little display have anything to do with the fact that I didn't take the initiative and make love to you in Houston?"

Jenny gasped and stopped dead. "That was a low blow, Matt."

"You set the rules for this game, baby. You've wiggled your cute little fanny at me one time too many."

Matt grasped the rope and began to gather it up

in his hands, pulling Jenny toward him. She didn't come willingly, or easily. She sat down and dug her toes in to resist, but there was never any question of who was stronger. Slowly but surely, Matt dragged her closer, until she was lying on the floor beside his bed and he was standing spread-legged over her. He dropped to his knees, straddling her waist, taking care not to touch her. He leaned over her with his weight braced on his palms on either side of her head. "All right, Jenny. Ask me for what you want."

Jenny lay rigid beneath him. She swallowed and said, "I want you to retract your review."

"What else do you want, Jenny?"

"Why are you doing this, Matt?"

"What else do you want?" he demanded, his voice harsh.

"Nothing, damn you!"

It took all Matt's willpower not to grab her by the shoulders and shake her. She wanted him. He knew she wanted him, yet she lay still beneath him, defiant, and all the more desirable because of her defiance.

"Matt... I..."

In that instant he knew she was going to give him what he wanted. And he was just as sure that he'd changed his mind about wanting it. Because if he took her now, he would have her for the moment, but he would lose her for a lifetime. Abruptly he stood and stepped away from her.

"Go to bed, Jenny."

"Matt, I—"

"Get the hell in bed before I change my mind!"

Jenny scrambled from the floor into her bed and yanked the covers up over her.

Matt lay down on his bed and stared at the ceiling. When he heard Jenny's muffled weeping he closed his eyes and gritted his teeth, forcing himself to ignore it. That woman was damned lucky. She had no reason to be crying, that was for sure. As many knots as she had him tied in, she ought to be laughing her fool head off.

Eight

A tug on the rope at her waist woke Jenny before dawn the next morning. She opened her eyes to the sight of Matt sitting fully dressed on the edge of his bed, staring at her.

"I need to make a trip over to see my editor today," he announced.

"All right," Jenny said, cautiously drawing the sheet up to her neck as an extra shield against Matt's steady gaze. "After class—"

"George is waiting for me right now."

Jenny sat up in bed, a frown furrowing her brow.

Matt looked haggard, as though he hadn't slept a wink. "Is there some emergency?"

Matt avoided Jenny's eyes when he answered, "You could say that."

"Oh."

"The cab is already waiting."

Jenny hurriedly dressed, wondering how she'd slept soundly enough to miss a call. Or had Matt called George? After what had happened between them last night, Jenny believed anything was possible. A shiver of alarm traveled down her back. Surely Matt wasn't going to back out of the project at this late date. Not after they'd managed to make it through all but the last showing.

Jenny's musings were left unresolved through the early morning cab ride to the offices of *Artist's World*. When they arrived, Matt stepped inside the threshold of George's office before turning to block Jenny's way. "You can have a seat out here. I may be a while." Then he dropped the extra length of rope between them on the carpeted floor so it would pass beneath the portal, and shut the door in her face.

Jenny stood there in disbelief for a moment, then sank into the comfortable chair that had obviously been placed outside George's door for just such a purpose.

What's going on, Jenny?

How should I know!

Do you think he's quitting?

Not without printing a retraction, he isn't!

Do you think that's why he's here to talk to George?

I don't know what to think. But if he knows what's good for him, he'd better not make me late for class.

Jenny followed the trail of rope from her waist to where it was mashed into the carpet beneath George's door. She listened for voices, but couldn't hear anything beyond the wooden partition. Whatever Matt was saying, he must be saying it in a normal tone of voice. That was a good sign, wasn't it?

Half an hour later, Matt opened the door. His jaws were tight, his eyes bleak. "Let's go," he said curtly.

Jenny stood and looked for George, who appeared momentarily in the doorway. "Hello, Jenny," he said with a friendly smile.

"Hello, George. How are you?"

"Are you going to stand there and gab all day?" Matt demanded.

"I think he wants to go," George said, giving Jenny's hand a reassuring squeeze.

Jenny turned to Matt. "Are we in a hurry?"

"You're the one with the 9:00 a.m. class," he reminded her.

"I guess we do have to leave. I'll see you soon, George."

"Sooner than you think," George murmured as Matt towed Jenny away.

"What did he want?" Jenny asked when they'd caught a cab and were on their way to the New School campus.

"I called him, he didn't call me."

Matt's jaws were still tight, and Jenny was determined to loosen them. "Well, what did you want from him?"

"I wanted out!"

Jenny's face paled until her golden eyes provided the only color.

"Are you satisfied now?" Matt glared at her and thrust a hand recklessly through his shaggy black hair. "I just wanted out."

"Oh." Jenny swallowed over the huge lump in her throat. "I take it George wouldn't let you quit."

"Hell, no! He threatened me with—"

"He threatened you? With what? How?"

"He's my boss, Jenny. He's got all the power he needs to make my life miserable."

"But George doesn't seem like the kind of guy who'd—"

"You don't know George Taplinger the way I do. Take it from me, George is one tough cookie."

"So you gave in to his threats, and that's why you're still here, tied to me."

Matt sighed. "That's about it."

Jenny thought she knew why Matt had wanted out of the project. But if he thought she'd teased him on purpose last night he was wrong. Maybe it would be best if they just got everything out in the open and talked about it.

"As long as you're stuck with me, why don't we just make a clean breast of everything that's bothering us about living with each other? You tell me what you want from me, I'll tell you what I want from you, and we'll do the best we can the rest of our time together to fulfill each other's expectations. How does that sound?"

Matt stared off into the shadowed canyon created by New York's skyscrapers. He pursed his lips ruefully and glanced at her from the corner of his eye. "That doesn't sound like a half-bad idea. Who goes first?"

They'd arrived at the school, and Jenny waited until Matt had paid the driver and they were walking to her class to continue. "I'll tell you what. Let's have a picnic in Central Park this afternoon, and we'll draw straws then to see who goes first.''

"You got it.''

As far as Jenny was concerned, Central Park was one of New York's greatest resources. It was a haven of nature in an unnatural setting. She spread a blanket on the grass and plopped down on top of it to unload the paper bag full of goodies she and Matt had picked up at a deli on the way.

When they'd devoured the sandwiches, chips and soda, she held up two straws and said, ''Short straw goes first.''

Matt chose the short straw. ''It figures.''

"All right. Let's hear it,'' Jenny said, stretching out on her side with her head held up by one hand. ''What's driving you nuts about living with me?''

"You mean aside from the fact I want to make love to you and can't?''

Jenny gulped. She was back in deep water, and she'd never been a very strong swimmer. ''Aside from that.''

Matt shrugged. ''A lot of little things, if you want to know the truth.''

"Like what?'' Jenny persisted.

"I'd like you not to nag me about leaving toothpaste in the sink.''

"I don't nag!"

"Do you want to hear what I have to say or not?"

Jenny sat up and ran her fingers across her lips like an imaginary zipper.

Matt rolled his eyes and continued. "I'd like to be able to smoke a cigarette without all those comments about how I'm going to die of cancer before I'm fifty."

"You will, you know," Jenny murmured. One look at Matt's thunderous expression prompted her to add, "Forget I said that."

"I want the light out at a decent hour."

"One o'clock is decent."

"Some people get up early in the morning to exercise."

"All right, then, I'll turn out the lights at twelve-thirty," Jenny suggested.

"Eleven."

"Midnight."

"Eleven-thirty," Matt compromised.

"That's an hour and a half earlier than I normally go to bed," Jenny sputtered.

"I can think of something a whole lot better to do with the time than read!" he growled.

"Like what?" she challenged.

"Like make love to you, Jenny."

"Why do you keep saying that?"

"Because it's true. The whole time you're lying there reading about some hero making love to some heroine, I'm lying there thinking about making love to you! And I'm here to tell you, it's a damned uncomfortable situation!"

"All right, Matt. I'll turn the light out at eleven-thirty."

"Just like that."

"Just like that. Is there anything else you'd like to say?" Jenny asked. "You seem to be on a roll."

"I'd...uh...I'd like you to wear something different for pajamas. Something that doesn't show off your legs." Matt's eyes followed the length of Jenny's long legs, from her ankles to her denim-clad thighs. "I'd prefer not to have so much temptation thrust in my path at bedtime."

Jenny's mouth was dry as she met Matt's heated gaze. "All right," she croaked. "You got it."

"Your turn, Jenny. What can I do to make the next ten days easier for you?"

"Wipe out the sink. Pick up your shorts. Don't smoke in..." Jenny found it hard to concentrate. Her eyes had caught on the tuft of black hair that showed above Matt's collar, then drifted down to the muscles in his forearms, and finally to the hard muscles beneath the soft cotton below his belt.

"Jenny?"

"Uh…what?"

"If you want to check me out, *Ms*. Smith, all you have to do is ask," Matt chided gently.

Jenny's face flushed bright red. "Good grief. I'm sorry, Matt. What were we? Oh, yes. What did I…I was going to ask…Oh, dear. I'd be pleased if you'd stick a bag on your head and cover up those sexy eyes and that smug grin. At least then I could think straight," she snapped.

Matt's amused chuckle at Jenny's totally flustered state soon built to a full-fledged guffaw.

When the ridiculousness of her request sank in, Jenny's good humor grew to match Matt's, until they were both rolling around on the blanket laughing uncontrollably.

By the time their howls had subsided to pleased giggles, they were lying side by side on their backs. Matt shifted to his side, and Jenny mischievously gave him another once-over.

Matt waited until she finished, then smiled and said, "Ah, Jenny, you're priceless. No wonder I love you."

A tense silence ensued as they both absorbed the significance of what he'd said.

"I know you didn't mean that the way it sounded," she said at last. She sat up and concentrated on straightening her blouse, which had pulled out of her waistband, exposing her abdomen.

"I meant it exactly the way it sounded."

Jenny's hazel eyes quickly searched Matt's face. The caring—and the passion—were both there. "You can't love me," Jenny protested. "We're like oil and water. We could never get along together."

Matt sat up and rested his forearms on his knees. "I'm not crazy about the situation, either. But there it is."

"This is impossible."

"You're telling me."

"I don't know what to say."

"You don't have to say anything, Jenny. I wasn't asking whether you returned my feelings—"

"But I do." She smiled sadly. "I don't know what we're moping about. Most couples would be overjoyed to find out they're in love with one another."

"Most couples never spend their first three weeks sleeping together in the same bedroom, forbidden to touch one another." Matt fingered the rope, which was looking as frayed as their tempers had become on occasion. "You do realize, Jenny, that once we cut this rope, we'll probably go in different directions and never see one another again."

Jenny swallowed past the painful lump in her

throat. "Uh huh." So...he might love her, but he wasn't going to let it go any further than that.

The uncomfortable silence was back.

"I guess we'd better go. The sun's about gone," Jenny said, busying herself with collecting the paper bags from the deli.

"Yeah. I guess we'd better."

They both stood and grabbed for the blanket, but Matt took it from her and shook it in the direction of the gentle breeze, before he gave it a casual folding.

"Will you be my date for the benefit on Saturday, Jenny?"

"What about Gerty?"

"I want to go with you."

"I don't know if that's such a good idea."

Matt pursed his lips in thought for a moment. "Look, you have to go whether you go with me as a date or not. So we might as well save the hassle of picking up and dropping off two more people."

For practical reasons, Matt's invitation made perfect sense. The problem was, it increased the intimacy between them at a time when he'd made it clear that their relationship would be over in ten days' time. For her own protection, Jenny's inclination was to refuse.

You only go round once in this life. Grab for the gusto!

Act in haste; repent at leisure.

A penny saved is a penny earned.

What does that have to do with anything?

I just wanted to see if you were paying attention.

I heard what you said; I just don't agree with you.

Better safe than sorry, huh?

I'm afraid so.

Matt was watching Jenny chew her lip in indecision, so he saw the moment when she finally made up her mind to refuse him.

"I'll go with you Saturday, of course, but I don't think we should call it a date," she said.

"If that's the way you want it, Jenny, that's the way it will be."

"That's the way I want it."

Jenny spent the next few days granting the requests Matt had made in Central Park. She wouldn't swear to it, but she thought he'd actually thrown his undershorts in the laundry basket one morning. And she hadn't seen a lick of toothpaste in the sink since Tuesday. She had no explanation for Matt's strange behavior, but it touched her more than she could say that he'd made the effort to change for her.

Not that he'd been an angel. He'd been notoriously smug when he'd smoked a cigarette in bed last night. She'd allowed him his moment of glory, then dumped the contents of the ashtray in the toilet and washed it in the bathroom sink. So maybe they still had a few problems that would have to be worked out. Could she be blamed for wishing?

And she was wishing hard, Jenny realized, for a miracle to happen, like in her romance novels. Matt would suddenly become the forceful yet sensitive hero who would sweep her off her feet and carry her away to the land of Happily Ever After. But he had given her no indication that that was going to happen. He'd been friendly, fun to be with, cooperative—but distant. And George Taplinger had helped him keep that distance.

On Tuesday evening they'd barely arrived home from the park when George knocked on the door.

"I have some business to discuss with Matt," he'd said.

Jenny had invited him in, and he and Matt had sat at the kitchen table and worked. They hadn't said much, and, bored, Jenny had finally fallen asleep on the couch. Matt had woken her after George had left, and they'd gone right to bed.

George's mysterious arrival immediately after the dinner hour "to discuss business" had repeated itself on Wednesday and Thursday. When Jenny had turned on the TV to watch Thursday night football, all pretense of work had been dropped, and Matt and George had joined her to watch the game. Once again, George stayed late, and by the time he left, Jenny and Matt dropped right into bed.

Jenny began to suspect what the two men must have discussed at the office on Tuesday morning. On Friday she had greeted George with a sardonic smile. "Hello. Here to act as guard dog again?"

George had blushed, but he hadn't contradicted her.

Matt had glared, as if daring her to say anything.

"If you'd brought your wife, we could have played some bridge. But since you didn't, why don't we play poker?" Jenny suggested.

By the end of the evening, Jenny was the big winner, with a total of forty-three toothpicks to Matt's forty-one and George's three. George had a terrible poker face, but he made a wonderful buffer. Thanks to his presence, she and Matt had made it through the last few evenings with a minimum of tension, sexual or otherwise. They only had to last seven more days without touching for Jenny to fulfill the requirements of her project.

It was late Saturday afternoon. Jenny had already showered and washed her hair, and now she was rifling madly through her closet, trying to find something to wear to the United Way benefit. Nothing looked right.

Matt was lying on his bed, his hands clasped comfortably behind his head, watching her. "What about the one you're holding in your left hand?"

Jenny held the orange, red and purple gown up in front of her and stared at herself in the full-length mirror behind the closet door. She frowned pensively. "I think it's a little too much."

"I vote for that dress I watched you making out of silk and velvet last week. You know. Vintage Jenny Smith Wearable Art—tons of textures, cool colors, diamonds, rubies and pearls."

Jenny laughed and put back the two dresses she'd been holding in order to pull out the outfit Matt had described. She'd been experimenting when she'd made it. One of her clients had asked for something daring, and Jenny had made this outfit. When she'd presented it to the client, the woman had said, "Darling, I said *daring*, not *decadent*." The client had been Jenny's size, so she'd brought it home. She hadn't ever foreseen actually wearing it, but then, it was a piece of art she'd created, so she couldn't very well throw it away, either.

Jenny held it up in front of her. "I don't know, Matt."

"Try it on."

"It doesn't have a back."

He grinned. "I won't tell. Come on. Try it on."

She disappeared behind her dressing screen and slipped out of her bathrobe and into the outfit. It fit as if it had been made for her. Jenny smiled to herself as she tugged on the part of the gown that had probably prompted the label of *decadent*. There was a man's white dress glove sewn at a provocative angle across the bodice, so that when the dress was worn, the glove cupped the wearer's right breast. Meanwhile, the back of the dress draped from the shoulders all the way to the waist, so no bra could be worn under the velvet bodice. A three-quarter length satin skirt hugged her from waist to mid-thigh, but had an enticing slit up the front to a point somewhere several inches above her knees.

If feeling sexy was decadent, then the dress fit her client's description, because the instant Jenny pulled the top up over her shoulders, she felt as though Matt were touching her. Heat pooled behind the satin caressing her belly, and her nipples budded beneath the velvet that shaped her breasts.

When Jenny came out from behind the screen, Matt had to force himself to stay on the bed. Her eyes were lambent with passion, and her walk… Her walk said her legs were shaky and it would take only his cooperation to put her on her back beneath him.

"That's quite an outfit, Ms. Smith."

"Why, thank you, Mr. Benson." Jenny walked all the way over to Matt and sat down beside him on the narrow bed.

"Whose glove is that?" he asked, reaching out with one hand to match the glove's grip, careful not to actually touch.

Jenny closed her eyes and leaned her head back, letting her hair fall down her bare back. "I wish it were yours, and that you were wearing it."

Matt jerked his hand away as though he'd been scalded and quickly slipped off the bed on the side opposite Jenny. "If you could bottle whatever that dress does for a woman, you could make a fortune," he said dryly. "I assume you've decided to wear it tonight."

Jenny curled up like a kitten facing him and said with a feline smile, "Yes, I think I will."

"Uh, if you don't mind, I'll take my shower now." He made a hasty exit, closing the bathroom door firmly between them. He used the entire time he was showering to preach a lesson in modest behavior to his libido. It was a totally wasted effort.

The instant he stepped out of the bathroom he was assailed by the scent of expensive perfume. Jenny

was sitting with her back to him, and he was treated
to the lovely sight of her bare back draped in dark
blue velvet. He followed the indentation of her spine
to the point where royal blue satin thwarted his
view.

At that moment Jenny turned and smiled at him.
She'd been at work on her makeup, and the huge
hazel eyes that had first attracted him to her were
sultry now. Bright red lipstick outlined her lips in a
pout, and gloss gave them a wet look. Her cheek-
bones had never appeared so high and proud. She'd
brushed her shoulder-length hair and let it hang free,
and the silky golden mass floated around her shoulders, begging to be touched. In fact, everything
about her begged to be touched. He grabbed his tuxedo and retreated into the steamy bathroom.

Jenny was so busy getting ready that she forgot
about Matt. When she finally turned around, he was
standing behind her, wearing his tuxedo. The contrast of the stark white shirt with his tanned skin,
and the black vest, coat and pants, was stunning.

She stood and turned to face him. "That's quite
an outfit, Mr. Benson."

Matt ate her up with his eyes. He knew that if
they didn't leave, he would have that outfit off in
the next two seconds. "Come on, Jenny. We'd better get going," he said curtly.

She felt the frisson of sexual awareness arcing between them and almost responded to it. But the desire in Matt's gray eyes was warring with something else she didn't recognize, so she turned with a swish of satin and led the way out the door.

They made quite an impressive couple when they arrived in the limousine Matt had rented at the hotel that was hosting the banquet. He had arranged to have his art supplies and easel set up earlier in the afternoon. Now he promptly took his place on the low camp stool behind the easel and left Jenny to her own devices. Almost immediately, one of the art patrons attending the benefit occupied the long-legged director's chair across from Matt and asked for a caricature.

Jenny stood at Matt's shoulder and watched in awe as an exaggerated version of the woman's features took form. Jenny marveled that he could work so quickly and effectively. In this case, he focused on the woman's hairdo and her smile. Both were already flamboyant, but under Matt's black-marker pen they assumed comical dimensions.

"Who does your hair?" he asked the woman.

"Simone's," she answered.

"You should ask her to put a little more curl in it next time," he said earnestly.

The woman laughed, since frizzy auburn curls

were already dripping off her head in clumps like hanging wisteria blossoms.

When Matt was finished there were chuckles and murmurs of approval from the crowd that had gathered, and the director's chair was quickly filled with another charity patron.

He worked until midnight without a break. Occasionally Jenny intercepted a glass of champagne from a passing tray and offered it to him, but he'd only take a sip and then set it aside. Jenny would finish the rest of the glass and grab another when she thought he might be thirsty again.

He was more than just a good artist, she thought as she watched him work for hour after hour. He had a way with people. Most left after five minutes in the director's chair with a smile on their faces, having happily parted with their one-hundred-dollar donation in exchange for a signed Matt Benson caricature.

Just before he was ready to quit for the evening, he coaxed Jenny into the chair. "Come on, Jenny. I want to do you."

"I don't have your sitting fee with me," Jenny demurred.

"I'll donate it. Come on, please sit for me."

Several of the patrons, including George Taplinger and his wife, urged her to comply. Laughing helplessly, she finally gave in. She couldn't imagine which of her features Matt would choose to exaggerate, but from the Cheshire cat grins on the faces of those who were watching him work, she wasn't going to be disappointed.

When Matt finished, he signed his name with a flourish and said, "You can look now."

Jenny was almost afraid to see how Matt perceived her, but because people were watching, she had no choice. Like Matt's other patrons, Jenny was pleased by his whimsy. He'd made her hazel eyes huge and sparkling with mischief; her breasts were full, and lovingly cupped by the white glove on her dress; and her legs were so long and gangly that from her waist down she could have passed for a giraffe.

Matt had been drawing for so many hours that he'd penned the full-length caricature of Jenny almost on reflex. When he stood back and looked at what he'd produced, he was stunned. He'd drawn a caricature, all right. There, preserved for posterity, was the stereotypical Matt Benson date—big-eyed, full-busted and long-legged. But Jenny was so much more than that!

Matt exchanged a quick look with George and knew that even if Jenny hadn't seen it, his boss had recognized the drawing for what it was.

"Jenny, I'll draw another one if you want. I'm so tired, I guess I—"

"No, Matt, it's perfect. You have a great eye and a vivid imagination. I don't know how you've lasted this long without collapsing."

Relieved that Jenny wasn't offended, he unbent enough to admit, "I'm beat. What do you say we head home?"

They said their goodbyes to George and his wife, as well as to the chairman of the benefit, who thanked Matt profusely for the contribution of his time and talent. Then they were on their way home in the limo.

Jenny settled back on the velvety seat and closed her eyes.

"You look tired, too," Matt said.

Jenny peered up from beneath lowered lashes, and her lips curved in a lazy smile. "Not really. But I think I may have had too much champagne. I seem to have this sort of... I don't know how to describe it...devil-may-care...attitude tonight."

Matt swore under his breath. "Jenny, don't do this to me."

The lazy smile broadened, and the lashes swept lower. "Don't worry, Matt. You're safe."

At least until we get back to my apartment, she added silently.

Nine

"What are you doing, Jenny?"

"I'm undressing."

"Then get behind the screen."

"No."

Matt knew he was in trouble. Disaster was staring him in the face. He tried to ignore her, but that was hardly possible under the circumstances. He was at the end of his rope. Unfortunately, Jenny was at the other end.

He watched as she unzipped her skirt and let it drop, revealing a lacy garter belt, silk stockings and skimpy bikini panties—all black as sin and twice as sexy.

She turned to face him wearing only the velvet bodice and the provocative feminine undergarments.

Matt swallowed hard.

Jenny took one step toward him, then another.

"Stop right there, Jenny," Matt commanded. "You've had a little too much champagne, and I don't want you doing something tonight you'll regret tomorrow."

Jenny smiled a predatory smile. "I know perfectly well what I'm doing," she purred. "As to whether or not I'll have any regrets tomorrow, well, I'm counting on you to make sure I don't." She took another step closer. There were only inches separating them now.

Matt's body went crazy. All his senses tuned in to the feminine signals Jenny was sending. The smell of her perfume, the sexy droop of her eyelids, the pout of her lower lip, her upthrust breasts, the jut of her hipbones and her wide-legged stance all combined to form an irresistible siren's call he was helpless to resist.

"There won't be any retraction, Jenny," he said, his voice harsh with need. "I want that understood now, before we go any further."

A shadow passed across Jenny's eyes, then disappeared. "No retraction. Okay. Now, can we put all that behind us and do what we've both been aching to do for nearly a month?"

Matt could hardly believe his ears. Jenny... aching? "Tell me what you want, Jenny."

"I want you, Matt. Touching me. Loving me. Deep, deep inside me." Jenny's eyes never left Matt's as she lifted her hands to slip off his jacket and loosen his tie. She unbuttoned his vest, then reached for the top stud of his shirt and removed it.

Well, you've done it now, Jenny. You touched him before the thirty days were up.

This was inevitable.

Excuses, excuses.

I love him.

As excuses go, that's not a bad one, but what about your project, Jenny?

I'm busy right now. Talk to me tomorrow.

Jenny's hands were trembling when she removed the second stud. When Matt reached up to help her, she captured his wrists and said, "I want to do it."

So, although his body was taut with desire, Matt stood perfectly still while Jenny slowly pulled the shirt from his trousers and removed the rest of the studs. When she was done, she slid both hands inside the opening she'd created and let her fingers play through his crisp black hair. She tested the muscled ridges of his chest and belly with her fingertips, then shoved the starched white cotton shirt and woolen vest off his shoulders so she could look at him. She leaned across the narrow distance that separated her from Matt to take one budding male nipple into her mouth and suck on it.

Matt groaned as the feel of Jenny's lips on his skin broke his control. He did what he'd imagined doing all evening: he fitted the imprint of his hand on the white glove that cupped Jenny's right breast. Jenny arched her breasts upward to meet his touch. With his other hand Matt pulled her hips into the cradle of his own, until their bodies, too, fit hand in glove. He thrust once against her, letting her feel the strength of his need. "Ah, Jenny, love, I want you, too."

Matt found Jenny's mouth and bit at the pouting lower lip that had so tantalized him over the past weeks. He tasted each bit of her mouth and the soft underside of her upper lip with his tongue before dipping inside. He teased her with his tongue, enticed her to meet him halfway, then captured her mouth, thrusting his tongue inside to taste her fully.

Jenny met Matt's ardor and matched it with her own. Her hips curved into his, rubbing against him, finding pleasure and seeking more. Her hands worked their way from his chest to his shoulders and thrust into his hair. She pulled his head down so she could reach his mouth more easily.

"I like the way you kiss," Matt said, as his lips drifted across Jenny's chin and down her throat. "Lots of little nibbles."

Jenny laughed. "You kiss kind of nibbly yourself."

"That's because you taste good," Matt murmured against her skin.

She tilted her head to give him better access to her neck, then shivered as his teeth nipped at her earlobe and his moist breath filled her ear. "I knew it would be like this," she murmured.

"Like what?"

"My heart is pounding so hard, I think it's going to burst."

Matt grinned and admitted, "Mine too. Here, feel." He took one of Jenny's hands and laid it against his heart. He stood back so he could see her eyes. They were lambent with need, shining with happiness. "It's time for bed, Jenny."

Jenny felt her heart, which she'd thought was already at full gallop, take off for the races. "I was planning to read a little," she teased.

"I'd like to suggest something better we can do."

Jenny laughed, a husky, sexy sound that sent a

shaft of fierce desire arrowing to Matt's loins. "I want to see you, Jenny."

Jenny reached up to pull the velvet bodice down, but Matt stopped her.

"I want to do it."

He didn't remove the bodice right away. Instead, he turned on the radio and pulled Jenny into his embrace, placing her arms around his neck. His hands roamed the bare expanse of her back, pressing her breasts into his chest. Meanwhile his mouth roamed her throat and teased her earlobes. Then his hands slipped down to her buttocks, clasping the silky panties and bringing her belly to meet his.

Jenny's whole body was awash with sensation. She sought Matt's skin with her mouth, returning the pleasure he gave, only to discover that the sucking and kissing and nipping fed her own pleasure.

Jenny didn't know when it had happened but suddenly she wasn't wearing her bodice any longer.

Matt whispered in her ear, "Your breasts are lovely, Jenny. So soft. So smooth." He bent his head to her and slid his tongue around the edge of a nipple, then sucked it into his mouth. Jenny's fingers thrust into his hair, holding him there. "Matt, you make me feel so much I thought I'd never feel again."

He pleasured her and himself, playing, teasing,

taunting, until Jenny was breathless with desire. She returned the favor, playing and laughing with him. He made a game of removing her black silk stockings, kissing his way down each leg to her foot. Then he unfastened the garter belt and skimmed it away. She was so bound up in touching him that it took a moment before she realized he'd removed her panties, as well. She grasped Matt's shoulders as his hands slid down her belly to the tops of her thighs and back up to the nest of curls that sheltered her femininity. For an instant she held her legs together, barring his way.

"Ah, Jenny, love, let me in," he coaxed.

His hands were gentle as they circled her concave belly, found her hipbones and then headed back again to the core of her. Jenny widened her stance slightly, and Matt's hand found what it sought.

She let her head fall back as she surrendered to temptation. His mouth found her breast again, and the combination of sensations took her breath away. "That…feels…so good," she moaned. She pushed against Matt's hand, arched against his mouth. And then she wanted more. Needed more.

Feverishly her hands fumbled at the zipper of his trousers. She had his pants halfway down his hips before he managed to stop her. "Jenny, wait."

"I can't wait," she moaned. "I want you inside me. Now."

Matt didn't argue; he simply helped her finish undressing him, then yanked down the sheets on his bed. He lifted her in his arms and laid her down, coming to rest on top of her. "This is where you belong," he said. "This is where you've always belonged."

His mouth came down on Jenny's, stopping any protest she might have made. Soon the passion that had carried them into bed brought them both to a point of need that was undeniable. Matt spread Jenny's legs with his thighs and thrust into her. She surged upward to meet him, so that he lodged himself deep inside her. They both moaned, satisfied sounds of mutual enjoyment.

Once inside her, Matt paused and raised himself on his arms. He brushed aside the sweaty curls on Jenny's forehead with his lips. "I'm yours now to do with what you will," he said.

Panting, Jenny managed, "I think you have that backward. But if my wish is your command, I'd like you to keep on doing what you're doing."

Matt chuckled. He backed away slightly and thrust again. "How's that?"

Jenny slipped a hand from Matt's buttocks down between his thighs and in response to her teasing touch he thrust again, harder this time. "Now you've got it," she said with a laugh.

In moments there was no more talking, no more laughing, no more thinking, only pleasurable moans and whispered words without meaning.

Jenny wrapped her legs around Matt and held on through the tumultuous lovemaking that followed.

Sweating and sated, they clung to one another, panting, attempting to regather lost wits and to quiet racing heartbeats. Matt rolled to his side, bringing Jenny with him. She pressed herself against him, not wanting to be separated from him yet.

He pulled the sheet up over them, then reached out and turned off the light. He squeezed Jenny in his arms and said, "Oh, Jenny, I love you! What are we going to do?"

"I don't know," she whispered. "I really don't know."

In another moment Matt was asleep. Jenny lay there wide awake, uncomfortable because the knot in the rope that circled her waist and still bound them together had slipped around between them. She tugged at it until she was comfortable, then put her arms back around Matt.

During the night his hold on her loosened, and she turned on her side, away from him. She closed her eyes in despair, lying awake in the quiet darkness until sleep finally claimed her.

When she woke in the morning she found that Matt had claimed her again. He'd laid a possessive arm around her waist and pulled her into his embrace, so that her buttocks nestled against his thighs.

"Good morning, sleepyhead," he murmured in her ear.

He tightened his hold, and Jenny could feel that he was hard and ready. "I've heard of starting the day with a bang," she quipped, "but this is ridiculous."

Matt laughed, his voice rough with need. "It should be no surprise that I want you again."

Jenny closed her eyes and sighed. "I want you, too, Matt, but I think we have some talking to do first."

She tried to free herself, but he held her snug against him. "There's no reason why we can't talk like this."

"I want to see your face," she objected.

He hesitated a moment, then released her. "All right. Let's talk."

Jenny scooted off the bed and retrieved her robe from the bathroom door. Matt settled for arranging the sheet at his waist. She walked back and sat at the foot of the bed.

The two of them simply looked at one another for a moment, searching for changes that the past night might have wrought.

"You look tired," Matt said at last.

"I couldn't fall asleep after...I couldn't sleep."

"Why not, Jenny? Do you have regrets about what happened between us last night, after all?"

Jenny fiddled with the length of frayed rope that lay on the tangled sheets. She opened her mouth to speak, then closed it again. At last she said, "I'll have to call and cancel the showing of *Separate but Equal* that was scheduled for this afternoon at the gallery in SoHo."

"I don't see why. We never untied the rope between us."

"But we didn't keep ourselves separated for the full thirty days. My project—"

"Your project aimed to prove that a man and a woman could be more to one another than sexual objects. What happened between us last night doesn't disprove that theory, it only reinforces it."

"I don't see how you can say that," Jenny protested.

Matt closed the distance between them, grasping Jenny by the shoulders and looking into her eyes. "I can say that because I love you, Jenny. You're much more to me than simply a sexy woman. Although you are pretty sexy." He gave her a quick, hard kiss on the mouth. "You proved what you wanted to prove. Believe it."

She looked down at her hands, which were still twisting the frayed cord. "All right, Matt. I'll hold the showing this afternoon, because I can see that at this point it would do my career more harm than good to cancel it. I've lost enough credibility with the New York art community as it is."

Jenny left unsaid the fact that there would be no retraction to improve her reputation. Yet she felt no regret for what she'd done. After all, life was more important than art—and the promise of a lifetime with Matt was well worth the sacrifice of the few days left of *Separate but Equal*. She gently shook herself free of Matt's grasp and scooted away a few inches. "Are you still planning to write a review of the performance here in New York?"

"I'll have to write something, Jenny." He tried to soften the effect of his words by explaining, "George would have my head if he didn't get his article after letting me have all this time off from work."

"Then I think it would be better if we didn't see one another after the performance until that obligation is fulfilled. I'll cut the rope when the performance is done, and we can go our separate ways."

Matt started to argue, but Jenny interrupted. "You can hardly expect to write a fair, impartial article if we're living together as lovers—and if we stay together for the next five days, you know that's inevitable." She laid a hand on Matt's arm. "Do what you have to do. Then we can see if what we seem to have found is really there, or if it's only an illusion that fades once we're not forced to remain in one another's company."

"It's no illusion for me, Jenny."

"I hope not, Matt." She chewed her lower lip for another moment before she asked, "Have you thought about what it would be like to spend the rest of your life living with me?"

Matt's gray eyes skipped away from her intense perusal. "We have some problems that have to be worked out. Every couple does."

When Jenny snorted, Matt met her gaze with a bold stare and said, "There isn't any reason why we can't resolve the differences between us. That is, if we're both willing."

"Oh, I'm willing," Jenny said with a wry smile. "I don't want to miss the chance of seeing a chauvinist and a feminist settle down together to live Happily Ever After."

"We have more in common than you think."

"Like what?"

"We each have a failed marriage in our past, with a partner who was wrong for us. We both want children. We both love art. We…" Matt searched for another significant similarity. "We both love football," he said at last.

Jenny sputtered, then laughed.

"Don't laugh. Think of all those football widows.…"

"And widowers," Jenny inserted.

"And widowers," Matt dutifully repeated. "We won't ever have to worry about spending Mondays, Thursdays and Sundays alone during football season."

"You're grasping at straws."

"I'm fighting for my life."

Jenny's features sobered. "Oh, Matt." She threw herself into his arms, no longer able to stand the separation she was forcing between them.

Matt tightened his arms around her. He'd write the damned review for George, and then he'd come back to claim his woman. He knew he'd sound like a caveman if he explained that to Jenny, so he didn't say anything more. She would find out soon enough that he had no intention of letting her go. The chauvinist pig and the feminist prig were going to become man and wife.

Ten

This collection of photographs is incredible, Patrick. I'd forgotten about that time Matt and I took a carriage ride through Central Park. And this one, with Matt working at his desk at *Artist's World*. I don't remember you taking it."

"You were asleep on the couch in his office," Patrick explained.

"Oh."

"Have you heard from him, Jenny?"

"No, I haven't. Not for the past week. Not since we cut the rope."

"Why don't you call him?"

Jenny excused the familiarity. After all, she and Patrick had certainly become more than a little familiar, thanks to their spontaneous date. In addition, she and Matt had seen Patrick often over the nearly four weeks of her project as he'd recorded various moments with his camera. Jenny flipped through the photographs and stopped at one that showed her cutting her way through the rope with a pocketknife. She'd insisted on calling Patrick to record the moment, even though they were five days short of spending the entire thirty days together.

Matt hadn't taken his eyes off her, and once the rope was cut he'd taken her in his arms and held her, just held her. Jenny flipped a photograph and there it was, in vivid color. Why hadn't he called?

"This week's copy of *Artist's World* should be on the stands by now. Would you like me to go out and get one for you?"

It took the touch of Patrick's hand on her shoulder to make her aware that he was talking to her. "What did you say?"

"I'm going out to get a copy of *Artist's World*. I'll be back in a flash. Don't go away."

Jenny sat on her couch and stared out the window of her apartment.

Well, Jenny, this is it.

I thought I told you to go away.

No more hiding. No more wondering. No more waiting.

I wasn't hiding.

Sure looks like it from where I sit. Why don't you call him?

Women don't call men.

That's a sexist remark, Jenny, and unworthy of you.

Get lost.

Patrick was back too soon for Jenny's comfort. He handed Jenny the magazine. "Here it is, Jenny. The review starts on page five. I think you're going to want to read it alone, so I'll be leaving."

There was nothing on Patrick's face to tell her whether the review was good or bad. But she took it as a bad sign that he wasn't hanging around to catch her reaction. Before she could protest that she didn't want to be alone at a time like this, he had picked up his equipment and his photographs and left her apartment.

"I'm here to see Matthew Benson."

The *Artist's World* receptionist had seen Jenny often enough to know who she was. "Ms. Smith. Um, it's nice to see you. I'm sorry, unless you have an appointment—"

"He'll see me. Call him."

The receptionist looked over her shoulder across the roomful of computers toward Matt's office. "He's still talking with Mr. Taplinger."

"There's a chair outside George's office. I'll wait for him there," Jenny said.

"But you can't—"

Jenny was past the receptionist before the woman could stop her. The receptionist started to call Matt and warn him that Jenny was on the way, but at that moment two lines on the phone rang, and she picked those up instead.

Jenny made her way to George's office. She slipped into the comfortable chair outside his door and crossed her legs to wait. That was when she realized the door wasn't closed. She didn't mean to eavesdrop, but it was hard not to hear everything they said.

"That was a great article you wrote on Jenny Smith," George said. "Worth every penny it cost me to have you gone for nearly a month. And that was some fancy footwork you did, fixing it so we didn't have to print a retraction."

"Jenny's in love with me."

"You told me a feminist prig like Jenny Smith wouldn't last ten seconds if she were tied to the right man. I guess you turned out to be the right man!"

"It was a little longer than ten seconds, George."

Jenny stuck her fist in her mouth to keep from crying out. How dare he! How dare he reduce their relationship to some cheap seduction!

"There are some things about me and Jenny I think you ought to know," Matt said.

"I'm all ears."

Jenny didn't wait to hear the rest. She jumped up from her chair and burst into George's office.

"You don't have to say another word!" she raged at Matt. Jenny turned to George and said, "I thought you were a nice man. I can see Matt was right. You're one tough cookie, all right—an honest to God crumb! As for you—" She whirled and poked her forefinger against Matt's chest, punctuating her speech by repeatedly jabbing at him. "You are the lowest worm, the slinkiest snake and the stinkiest stinker it has ever been my misfortune to love!"

She whirled back to George again. "I'm sure a man of your editorial caliber will want to give me equal time to express my opinion of the days I spent tied to Matt Benson. Send a photographer to my apartment in an hour. I'll have a piece of performance art ready for him to shoot!"

She was too furious to cry. The crying didn't come until she was on the subway home. How could she have been so wrong about Matt? After she'd read his review of *Separate but Equal*, she'd been so sure he'd changed! But it had all been lies. She practically ran from the subway to her apartment. She'd show the whole world what Matthew Benson was really like!

Jenny gathered the materials she needed to present *Woman in her Natural State*, made the appropriate changes in her costume and sat down in the living room to wait for the photographer to arrive.

She'd barely gotten comfortable when the knock came. She undid the last lock and opened the door to find Matt standing on the other side.

"You weren't expecting me?" he asked when he saw her stunned expression.

She tried slamming the door in his face, but he stuck his foot inside. There was no contest. In another moment he was inside the apartment, with the door closed behind him.

"What the hell are you doing opening the door to some stranger dressed like that?" he demanded. "At least you've got something in your hand you can use to protect yourself."

"I happen to be dressed in a costume," Jenny snarled. "And this—" she took the steam iron in her hand "—this is part of my performance art project."

Matt took the time to really look at what she was wearing. The black negligee wasn't quite see-through, but it skimmed the margin of decency. At her waist she'd tied a red batiste apron. In her right hand she held an iron, and in her left hand a spatula. "What do you call this—this outfit?" Matt demanded.

"This is *Woman in her Natural State*."

Matt stared for a moment before he burst out laughing. "That's a good one, Jenny. That's really funny."

"I wasn't trying to be funny," Jenny snapped. "I was trying to show the world how Matt Benson perceives the female sex!"

"Then you'd better get it right!" he retorted, incensed by her revelation.

Before Jenny knew what had happened, Matt had scooped her up in his arms and carried her into the bedroom. He dropped her onto the bed he'd used and stretched out on top of her, holding her down with his weight. "*Now* you have *Woman in her Natural State*. This is where you belong, Jenny. In my bed, with me on top of you."

"You chauvinist jerk!"

"How can you call me a name like that after all the *liberated* things I wrote in my review of your project?" he demanded.

"All I had to do was listen at the door when you talked to George."

"When *I* talked to *George*? I didn't say a damn thing. George was doing all the talking. And what were you doing listening at the door, anyway?"

"I was there to thank you for your *kind* review. If I'd only known what you really thought! What was that review, Matt? A salve for your conscience? You ruined my project—"

"*I* ruined your project?" Matt asked incredulously. "Just who seduced whom?"

"I heard George say you didn't think I'd last ten seconds with the right man!"

"You lasted a hell of a lot longer than that, as you very well know!" Matt raged.

"You said there were things you wanted to tell him about our relationship. How could you, Matt? How could you tell him—"

Matt ended her tirade by closing her mouth with a kiss. Jenny didn't make it easy. She fought him, and, of course, he'd forgotten about the iron.

Unfortunately, Jenny had forgotten too, and she accidentally hit him with the iron, half stunning him. She dropped the iron and spatula on the floor, then reached up to frame his face. She looked deeply into his dazed eyes to see whether she'd caused some kind of concussion. "Oh, Matt, I'm sorry. Are you all right? I didn't mean to hurt you."

Matt moaned and dropped his head on Jenny's

breast. His head hurt, but it was well worth the pain to have Jenny concerned about him again. Somehow she'd overheard his conversation with George and misconstrued the whole thing.

"Jenny?"

"What, Matt?"

"You interrupted me in George's office a moment too soon."

"Matt, I—"

He kissed her again.

This time Jenny didn't fight him. It couldn't be good for a man with a concussion to fight, she thought.

The next time Matt came up for air, he put a fingertip across Jenny's mouth to keep her silent and said, "I was about to tell George that not only did you love me, but that I loved you, and I was going to ask you to marry me."

Jenny grabbed Matt's finger and said, "You were? You do? You are?"

"I love you, Jenny. Will you marry me?"

"Yes. Oh, yes!"

They lay there grinning at each other for several moments before it occurred to either of them that he had just tied himself for life to an unrepentant feminist.

"Is this going to work?" Jenny asked, voicing her doubts. "Are we going to be happy together, Matt?"

He brushed a wisp of hair from her forehead. "There are never any guarantees in life, but we have a lot going for us. We can make it work."

"I think we should work on something else right now," she said.

"What's that?"

"Woman in her Natural State."

"Oh, yes. Where were we?"

"You said my place was here, in bed, with you on top."

"And I was right, of course. The husband is always right, Jenny. If you'd just learn that lesson—" He laughed when Jenny chucked him in the ribs. "Did you like the review, Jenny?"

"It explained a lot about how you were feeling, what you were thinking, things I guess it was easier to write than to say."

Matt quoted into her ear, "Women aren't only angel food cake, they're also meat and potatoes. To treat a woman as no more than dessert is to miss having a full meal."

Jenny grinned. "That was the nicest food metaphor you've ever written." She caressed his shoulders and let her hands drift down the curve of his spine to the firm flesh at his waist. "But the part I liked best was where you said that I might currently be a liberated woman, but you were hoping I'd get shackled soon,'' Jenny said with a chuckle. She slipped her hands down to find his hard, excited flesh.

Matt felt his body tauten with need at her touch. He brushed the edge of his hand across her breast and watched her nipple peak beneath the negligee. She blushed becomingly, and their eyes met with a warmth that made him quiver with need.

''I have a piece of performance art I'd like to work on with you,'' he said.

Jenny tilted her hips up to meet his thrust. ''What did you have in mind?''

''How about something like, *And Baby Makes Three*?''

Jenny smiled. ''That sounds fine. That sounds wonderful. That sounds—''

Matt closed her mouth with a kiss.

*   *   *   *   *

SPECIAL EDITION

Stories of love and life, these powerful novels are tales that you can identify with— romances with "something special" added in!

Fall in love with the stories of authors such as **Nora Roberts, Diana Palmer, Ginna Gray** and many more of your special favorites—as well as wonderful new voices!

Special Edition brings you entertainment for the heart!

SILHOUETTE®
Desire®

Do you want...

Dangerously handsome heroes

Evocative, everlasting love stories

Sizzling and tantalizing sensuality

Incredibly sexy miniseries like **MAN OF THE MONTH**

Red-hot romance

Enticing entertainment that can't be beat!

You'll find all of this, and much *more* each and
every month in **SILHOUETTE DESIRE**. Don't miss these
unforgettable love stories by some of romance's hottest
authors. Silhouette Desire—where your fantasies will
always come true....

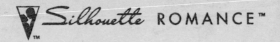

What's a single dad to do when he needs a wife by next Thursday?

Who's a confirmed bachelor to call when he finds a baby on his doorstep?

How does a plain Jane in love with her gorgeous boss get him to notice her?

From classic love stories to romantic comedies to emotional heart tuggers, **Silhouette Romance** offers six irresistible novels every month by some of your favorite authors! Such as...beloved bestsellers **Diana Palmer, Annette Broadrick, Suzanne Carey, Elizabeth August** and **Marie Ferrarella**, to name just a few—and some sure to become favorites!

Fabulous Fathers...Bundles of Joy...Miniseries... Months of blushing brides and convenient weddings... Holiday celebrations... You'll find all this and much more in **Silhouette Romance**—always emotional, always enjoyable, always about love!

WAYS TO UNEXPECTEDLY MEET MR. RIGHT:

♡ Go out with the sexy-sounding stranger
   your daughter secretly set you up with
   through a personal ad.

♡ RSVP yes to a wedding invitation—soon
   it might be your turn to say "I do!"

♡ Receive a marriage proposal by mail—
   from a man you've never met....

These are just a few of the unexpected
ways that written communication
leads to love in Silhouette Yours Truly.

Each month, look for two fast-paced, fun and
flirtatious Yours Truly novels
(with entertaining treats and sneak previews
in the back pages) by some of your favorite
authors—and some who are sure to
become favorites.

YOURS TRULY™:
Love—when you least expect it!

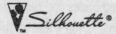

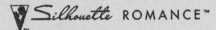